FEAR
False Evidence Appearing Real
by
James Leslie Payne
ISBN: 978-1-9997646-8-5

All Rights Reserved.
No reproduction, copy or transmission of the publication may be may be made without written permission. No paragraph or section of this publication may be reproduced copied or transmitted save with the written permission or in accordance with the provisions of the Copyright Act 1956 (as amended)
Copyright 2017 James Leslie Payne
The right of James Leslie Payne to be identified as the author of this work has been asserted in accordance with the Copyright Designs and Patents Act 1988.
A copy of this book is deposited with the British Library.

Published by

i2i PUBLISHING

i2i Publishing. Manchester.
www.i2ipublishing.co.uk

For Mary

"My insides are turned inside out; Spectres of death have me down. I shake with fear. I shudder from Head to foot.
Psalm 55:4

Introduction

I have a difficult confession to make, I'm not a writer! How do I know? I've read real writers' words, words that are smart, colorful, rich like a soft white angelic symphony, words that conjure up amazing thoughts in my cerebral cortex and inspire me. No, not inspire me; they transport me to a place I'd never known before. Like the time I went to a Leonard Cohen concert and heard a twelve-string guitarist named Maas make sounds that I didn't know guitars could make. It made me think of Godly things, higher things, and inspirational things. Let me give you an example; describing the horror and fire of war the writer Anthony Doerr pens *'a holocaust of scarlet and carmine.'* Rachel Joyce, in her novel the *Unlikely Pilgrimage of Harold Fry* describes windows on a dark night as *'buttery squares of light'*. Beautiful words. Oh, how I wish I could think and write like that but alas I cannot. I seem locked in a brown, square and straight-forward story-telling fashion. On that true confession my story telling begins.

Fear is an odd word. Someone told me that it stands for 'false evidence appearing real'. That seemed profound to me since my life's experience seemed to prove that to be true. I've watched people make incredibly important, life-changing decisions based on fear. They don't think about the outcome. They just want to escape the fear and dread that they are facing at that moment. Very often the outcome is worse than the fear they fled. I've often wondered where they'd be if instead of running away, or taking the least line of resistance to get away from the thing that frightened them, what would happen if they stood still and looked into the Abyss. Would it really have been as bad as they thought? I'm not sure, however I am sure that making decision on F-E-A-R, which to my knowledge is indeed 'false evidence appearing real' has frightening consequences.

James Leslie Payne

Contents

Chapter 01	Poor Choices	9
Chapter 02	Telling stories	13
Chapter 03	What is Jewish?	19
Chapter 04	Escape to sanity	23
Chapter 05	Banged up	28
Chapter 06	Rainy night	32
Chapter 07	Stark fear	42
Chapter 08	Awash in shoes	45
Chapter 09	Fear had found her	56
Chapter 10	The favour	59
Chapter 11	Texas	65
Chapter 12	Relentless	72
Chapter 13	Acclimate	79
Chapter 14	Running scared	88
Chapter 15	Safe place	93
Chapter 16	Change time	100
Chapter 17	Who's kidding who?	105

Chapter 18	Unexpected encounters	109
Chapter 19	A new creature	116
Chapter 20	Noddy in Toyland	120
Chapter 21	I'm still here!	125
Chapter 22	Impossible	135
Chapter 23	Back to the Rob	145
Chapter 24	End of the line	150
Chapter 25	'eaven elp us!	155
Chapter 26	The way you remember	162
Chapter 27	Reality	172
Chapter 28	.44 Magnum	178
Chapter 29	The comeuppance	182
Chapter 30	Forgotten	192
Chapter 31	Back to Hill Country	197
Postscript		198

Chapter #1 *Poor Choices*

"Come on, off to school Jimmy, you'll be late if you don't get a move on."

"Aw Mum I'm tired and I don't feel very well. Can I stay home today?"

"No you bloody can't, now get cracking and give your face a wash and then you'll feel better about going to school."

"I'm so tired."

"I know son, it's my fault for allowing you to stay up so late but you have to go to school, now come on!"

The boy was blonde and his hair was matted down from sleeping soundly, especially at the back of his head, which he couldn't see in the mirror as he splashed semi-warm water onto his face. His mother fussed over him and she spit on to her hand and tried to slick down the offending hair, but to no avail. Her long brunette hair hung down into his face and she worked on the back of his head trying to make him look presentable. She watched her boy walk down the lane way toward the school. It was only 3 short blocks. She told herself that she must stop keeping him up so late. She was so lonely for real affection and company plus she loved reminiscing about her family. No one except her boy wanted to hear her stories. He loved them for two reasons, first he just loved those stories and secondly it kept him from having to go to bed which was his most hated thing in the world. His mind couldn't rest as he thought about the same thing every night. *Dying*. The blackness of it gripped him so tight that he wasn't sure he could breathe sometimes. The fear rolled over him and he cried from the very visceral fear of being dead, being in the ground from, not 'being' at all. He hated and feared night time and bed time.

Mary returned to her housework. She was a nervous woman that lost herself in housework. The bedroom door opened and out lumbered her husband; he was always late getting out of bed, usually from the beer the night before. He was an unmotivated man that didn't think much, he just reacted out of his emotions and limited intellect. She watched him stumble to the toilet, his underwear was stained front and back and his stomach protruded and he hadn't shaved for more than three days. He had no job or any prospects of one. She wondered why she had settled for this and then the hair on the back of her neck stood up as she remembered that it was her fault. She was the one that fell in love with that smooth talking, good looking dandy and she allowed herself to get pregnant and this obtuse man was the only viable option open to her. It seemed like a way out at the time but now she was feeling short changed as she watched him disappear up the hallway with a distinct brown stain making its way up the back of his undergarment. He never spoke to her or even looked at her. The bedroom door closed and then immediately opened again.

"Shouldn't you be at your job?" He bellowed at her.

"Yes, I'm heading off as soon as I finished the washing up." She'd hoped he'd offer to finish the job, but she knew better.

As she reached for the tea towel she noticed a cigarette burning at the end of the counter. She had turned it around so that the hot end was hanging over the end of the counter and some of the ash had fallen on the floor. She tutted as she saw the many burned stains on the Formica counter that she'd forgotten, and they had burned into the counter. She reached for the still burning cigarette and drew hard on it to get the last of the smoke to fill her lungs. She couldn't really afford to smoke but she was totally addicted. It seemed to placate her nervous disposition. On her way out the door to catch the #161 bus to her factory job, she grabbed her warm coat and a heavy woollen scarf. The factory-made boxes, mostly cardboard, but some old wooden type boxes too. The shift was over at half past 4 in the afternoon. Then Mary made her way back to the #161 bus for the trip home and her other job, pulling pints at the Royal Oak. She knew most of the people that frequented that pub, after all it was the local to so many of her neighbours. Her feet hurt and arms ached from pulling and carrying so many pints of Double Diamond Ale, she was relieved to hear the landlord bellow, "Last call." She scurried home to find her husband out, as he was most evenings, drinking or who knows what, but she really didn't care at all. Jimmy was asleep in the chair with a half-eaten piece of toast that had fallen onto the floor, butter side down making a mess on her clean floor. He was far too big to carry into bed so she whispered softly in his ear until his eyes opened marginally and she coaxed him into getting up and she lovingly guided him into his bed.

She wanted him to be older so that she could get him to stay up again and drink hot sweet tea with her and reminisce with him. She wanted him to know that this wasn't supposed to be their lot in life. She came from good people, kindly people, and God-fearing people. This place they were in and the man that found themselves fallen in with was a terrible mistake, made by her fearful choices or lack of choices. She drifted off to sleep until at some point her husband pulled the warm covers back and threw himself upon her. She just closed her eyes, turned her head away from the smell of stale beer and cigarettes and his rough face and dreamed of the gentle love of her family until the ordeal was over.

Mary only worked three nights a week and never on the weekends at the pub. She hurried home on Saturdays from her factory job to make a nice dinner for her boy and spend time with him. She bought a weekly Beano comic at the corner sweet shop and hid it in her shopping bag.

"Hello, my Jimmy." He looked up from the telly and smiled at her. He was sure he had the most beautiful Mom in the world. She always had a smile for him and seemed to defend him in every circumstance.

"Where's my comic?" the boy asked.

"Comic, what comic?" she teased. Then with her wide grin she pulled the boy's comic from her shopping bag and he knew she hadn't forgotten him.

The coal was burning in the hearth of the front sitting room, the washing up all finished from the evening meal. The boy knew that his Mum had taken a cup of tea into the sitting room and was waiting for him. He took up his position in his usual spot and warmed his hands on the fire burning gently in the fireplace. She looked at him and smiled, "What story tonight my fine young man?"

"Mum, please tell me the one about great granddad and the Queen's funeral."

"Ok, my boy I'll tell you everything I can remember about it, but let's get another cup of tea first."

Chapter #2 Telling Stories

As the bridle stuck in the horse's mouth it raked across its teeth which made an awkward scraping noise. It didn't seem to fit as it was supposed to. The animal's eyes widened in terror. It reared back as if it knew instinctively that its usual rider possessed a quick temper, which usually led to cruel pokes and worse if things didn't go his way. The private was irritated and embarrassed, a dangerous combination. He picked up a stout stick and leaned back to teach this horse a lesson or vent his anger, no one was sure. A lightening hand blocked the blow and then another hand, as swift and sure, grabbed the young man's throat. A face as strong as the red hair it bore moved slowly but forcefully toward the private's face. He was trembling and had already started to sweat. "That animal would carry you into battle with courage and grace, the likes of which you'd never understand if he's asked. He'd die doing it and you want to treat him like a punching bag! You are a useless excuse of a human being. If I ever catch you being cruel to this beast, I'll beat you. I promise you, it will be a beating you'll never forget!" James Hunter Yeoman, the Sergeant Major had spoken and when he spoke everyone listened. He was from Aberdeen in Scotland and some wondered how a short man from the wilds of Scotland could have ended up in this position on this very day. James Hunter Yeoman was to be the lead rider in the saddest, proudest and most important of days, Queen Victoria's funeral procession!

The red-headed Sergeant loved the smell of the horse barns; he smiled when he thought of the reason why. It was the horse shit that gave the barn its dominant smell but it was the combination of horse sweat, brass polish, leather polish and of course horse manure that gave it that decidedly pungent smell. As he walked away he turned to the cruel private, and said, "I've heard of your way with these beasts and either you change your tune laddie or I make sure you're out of the unit and the army for good with the beating for good measure young man, are we clear?"

"Yes, Sergeant Major, very clear, sir." As Yeoman walked away, the private said to another solider in the next horse stall, "I'd like to meet him without his stripes on his arm, the short bastard would be sorry he'd ever talked to me that way." The other fellow laughed and said, "You've obviously no idea who you're dealing with do ya? Yeoman is one of the nicest blokes you'll ever come across but he's not to be messed with, especially if you're buggering about with the horses. He absolutely loves and protects them and he'd make mincemeat out of you. The story goes that at 5 years old he was given away to a wealthy farmer 'cause 'is family couldn't afford to feed him. The horrible git of a horse foreman that worked for the farmer beat him black and blue for the smallest mistake or sometimes just for sport. Yeoman suffered it for many years until he joined up. He went back to the landlord's horse barns and told the foreman that he'd forgiven him. The foreman spit in his face but before the foreman had time to respond Yeoman hit him once, broke his jaw and knocked him out cold. He is very kind but at the same time he's fearless. It's a strange combination. I'd follow his orders if I were you. I've heard other stories about him in battle. 'No fear' Yeoman is his nickname. The men that have fought with him told us it's as though he is not afraid to die." The young man decided to be silent after this latest warning. He did not want to be ejected from the Royal Horse Artillery. He didn't care in particular for horses. He just wanted to ride instead of walk and he needed to be in the army with a steady income and security so he yielded to the red-headed Sergeant Major.

It was cold and wintery outside. Grey, low clouds made everyone feel even more miserable than they already did. February 2nd 1901, this was the day that they were to escort their Queen to where she'd lie in state. She wasn't just the Queen. She was not just the head of state. She was the reason for the army, and she was the 'Mum Queen'. They loved her and the force she'd been in England, across Great Britain and all over the commonwealth. She made them all proud to be English; most would lay down their lives for her. After all, she spent her life in pursuit of making Great Briton as great and powerful as it had ever been.

She died two days earlier while at Cowes on the Isle of Wight. Word had dribbled down from the medical army brass that she'd had a stroke and died with her family around her. Today was the day all of England was to say the final goodbye, and James Hunter Yeoman was to be the lead horseman in this procession, the saddest and yet the most proud day of his young life. James was born in 1876 in rural Scotland not far from the city of Aberdeen. His father was a crofter; which meant that he farmed a small piece of land. Most of the bounty went to the landlord. Joseph, his father, was a sickly man that was never able to work the land or really able to provide for his son or his family. James was sent to live with his Grandfather, a successful crofter that had somehow become a landlord, with servants and livestock, so James was taken in but as a horse boy. He worked in the barns with the beasts and was given no special treatment; he never told anyone that the landlord was his grandfather.

"Sergeant Major Yeoman,"
"Yes sir?"
"Are your men ready for the day at hand?"
"Yes sir."

"Then let's get started for the trip to St George's Chapel. Let the men ready themselves for the task at hand."

"Yes sir," answered James Hunter Yeoman. Lieutenant Goldie was in charge of S Battery of the Royal Horse Artillery. He was a career solider and treated most of the enlisted men well; most respected him unless he was under the influence. He was a sloppy drunk, who couldn't handle his drink. The men in his battery stayed away from him if he was drinking because of the dichotomy caused by respecting him sober and embarrassed by his behaviour while drinking. This day he was most definitely dead sober and in fine form. It was Lieutenant Goldie that had recommended Yeoman to be the lead horseman on this, the most important of occasions. They reached Windsor station and waited in the miserable cold for what seemed like an eternity. The men were stamping their feet to keep the cold at bay and the blood flowing in their feet and legs. The horses were getting more and more skittish the longer the wait. Snow started to fall and even started to build up in spots.

"How are the men holding up?" asked Goldie to his Sergeant Major.

"They are fine sir. This cold is a small price to pay for the privilege of being a part of sending off the greatest Queen," his voice cracked, "England will ever see".

"Well said Yeoman, I'm not feeling the cold as much either."

Lieutenant Goldie touched Yeoman on the shoulder as a sign of thanks for those well-chosen words and turned, calling out for his Lieutenant of the guns, P.W. Game. "Lieutenant Game, are your guns ready?" Part of the funeral cortège included an 81-gun salute and that was the responsibility of Lieutenant Game.

"Aye, sir we are ready to go," shouted back the young lieutenant. It was time.

The weather hadn't got any better, if anything it had become colder and more snow was sticking on the street. The Royal coffin was placed on the gun carriage. The drums began to roll and the noise was exacerbated under the train station's metal roof. As the horses took up the strain, an eyelet hole on the splinter bar attached to the harness broke and violently struck the horse in the rear hock and the horse plunged. "We can fix it. It's a small matter," shouted James. "Let's get the horses out of the way and fix the eyelet hole on the splinter bar." Before they had a chance to do anything the naval detachment, as though without any direction, took hold of the gun carriage's drag ropes and pulled the coffin on the gun carriage to St George's Chapel where the Queen's own Grenadier Guards stood in solemn watch over their Queen's coffin as it laid in state.

Lieutenant Goldie was beside himself with humiliation; his greatest fear was being realized, disgracing his uniform, letting down his unit, his commanding officers and his new King, Edward the VII. Everyone just stood looking at each other not knowing what to say or what it might mean. James tried to get his men back on task but it was too late to save the day. It has been lost to circumstances beyond their control.

Later that evening as he took care of the last of his men and horses in the horse barracks, he stood outside and lit his worn pipe. It didn't take, so James tamped down the ashes and tobacco left in the bowl and lit another match, this time he drew hard and he could feel tobacco catch and soon he had a smooth stream of pipe smoke to fill his lungs and soothe his mind. All that afternoon and evening all of the talk was of the muddle that today had become. Some said they were 'in' for it and others spoke of humiliation for themselves and the legendary Royal Horse Artillery. Most didn't know what to think other than the realization that at their most critical moment in history they failed, unable to fulfill their solemn duty.

As James clutched his pipe and pulled one last time before he did his final rounds of the stables he heard the click of boots coming down the gangway. He quickly stuffed his still lit pipe is his nearest pocket and waited for the officer wearing those clicking boots to appear. It was Lieutenant Goldie and he was wearing the biggest grin that Yeoman had ever seen on him. Yeoman snapped to attention. "At ease Yeoman, at ease man, I've news. I've just come from the officers club, where I was approached by Colonel Read, who'd received word from the King himself that no blame should be borne by anyone for today's debacle. In fact, the King himself was close enough to see what happened and he said nothing could have prevented it. He also said that your emotional reaction moved him and he wants our regiment to lead the last of the procession from Albert Memorial chapel to the Frogmore Mausoleum at Windsor Castle. What's more, James, he's asked for you to lead that procession."

James was shocked, first that his Lieutenant would call him by his Christian name, and then the King asked for him to lead the cortège. "The King asked for me, why me?" Yeoman asked. "Because of the concern you showed at the train station when things went awry." Lieutenant hurriedly shook Yeoman's hand and quickly raced off to tell others. James found his still warm pipe and tried to light it again but this time it wouldn't catch. There was too much ash and not enough tobacco in the bowl, so he smiled and shook his head at the unexpected turn of events and went to do his final rounds for the night!

Chapter #3 *what is Jewish?*

Her husband came home at 2 o'clock in the morning and found his wife and her son, not his son, asleep in chair in the front parlour with the last of the burning coals smoldering in the grate, along with empty tea cups on the floor. He grunted his dissatisfaction and then simply walked away, went into his bedroom and fell onto the bed and started to snore.

As the light came in through the tops of the parlour windows Mary awoke with a fright and wondered where she was and why she was asleep in a chair. She looked over and saw her boy sound asleep and then realized where she was. It was cold. The only source of heat was the fireplace grate and it had long since exhausted the last of the coal. She got up and found a woollen blanket and covered her boy thinking that he looked more than comfortable where he was. She made her way to her bedroom but her huge man of a husband was laid out spread-eagled, face first across the bed which gave her no room. So she made her way to her son's room and snuggled into his small single bed with the candlewick bedcover. She pulled the covers up to her chin and started to feel her body heat build up under the covers almost immediately. That was the last thing she remembered until again she awoke with a fright. "Where are the bloody aspirins?" he bellowed. "My bloody head is killing me and my mouth feels like the bottom of a bird cage, full of sand and shit!" Mary thought *how crude* but ran as fast as she could to the last place she remembered having aspirins. No aspirins, she panicked and tried to think through the sleepy haze. Where did she put them? Just as she was searching her brain she heard her boy call for her.

"Mum, mum where are you?"
"I'm here, son, in the kitchen."

"Never mind that f'ing kid of yours gets those bloody aspirins." *The bed side cabinet*, it dawned on her where she had put the painkillers. She ran and retrieved them and handed them to her very unappreciative husband, who then asked for a drink. "Get yourself a drink of water from the tap." He scowled at her with a threatening look.

Mary decided that she needed to explain herself, "I know you have a headache but I'm trying to look after the boy and I've just woken up."

"Your boy you mean. Let me remind you that little bastard is just that, a bastard, and the only reason that you're living in a warm house is because of me, so when I ask you for a drink you might want to get it for me, got it?"

She just melted out of the room and kept looking at the floor. She took the boy and held him tightly. "What's the matter Mum? Why is he so angry and cruel to us? What have we done to make him like this to us?"

She whispered quietly, "Don't worry darling, don't worry." She looked over her shoulder to make sure he had returned to his bed to nurse his aching head and not to vent his unreasonable anger at her and her boy.

Her husband lumbered off to the pub in the afternoon after mumbling about a 'hair of the dog that bit him'. The boy didn't understand but was grateful that fear left when the big man did.

"Mum, what will we have for our dinner?"

"How about some toast with marmite and tomato soup?"

"Oh Mum that's sounds smashing can we sit in front of the telly and eat our soup?"

"Yes of course my love we can."

"I love dipping my bread in tomato soup it tastes so good, thanks Mum."

"You are a sweet boy, my darling." They had the telly playing while they ate their meal, but never watched it.

They just chatted like two old friends. After Sunday Night at the Palladium was finished Mary tidied up the supper plates and bowls and made a nice cup of tea and brought it into the front living room and gave her boy a cup with lots of milk and sugar. He smiled at her, knowing what was coming next.

"Mum."

"Yes my boy" answered his mother.

"You always talk about great Granddad but you never tell stories about great Gran, why not?"

"We'll it's complicated. You see Gran is...hmm...different."

"What do you mean, different?"

"Well, what does different mean to you?"

"Different means not the same as me."

"Yes, that's right. Do you remember Mr. Levi Bender?"

"Yes, the man who lives on the next street over who wears the funny hat with long beard."

"Yes, that's him, well he is Jewish and he's different to us."

"Is it because of his long beard and funny hats?"

"No, that's not the reason. He doesn't believe in Jesus. Well great Gran is Jewish."

"Great Gran doesn't wear those hats that Mr. Bender wears."

"No, I know she doesn't but she is Jewish."

"Mum, I still don't know what Jewish is."

"OK, this is going to be harder than I thought it would be. You know at Christmas time and Easter we go to church, and pray to Jesus?"

"Yes".

"Well Jewish people go to a different church. Their church doesn't believe in Jesus."

"Does Great Gran go to that church?"

"No she doesn't go to any church, but if she did go to church she would go to the Jewish church."

"Does she believe in God?"

"Yes of course she does. Now that's enough, Jimmy, you've got me all in knots with these questions. Great Gran is different to us but we love her just the same, and please don't ask her about being Jewish."

"Why? Is she shy about being Jewish?"

"Yes son, I think she is. Some people don't like Jewish people."

"Some people don't like my Great Gran because she is different, that doesn't seem right Mum."

"I know son, it doesn't seem right does it?"

"If Great Gran is Jewish and Great Grandad isn't, how did they meet each other. Come to think of it great Grandad must like Jewish people because he really likes Great Gran."

"Your Great Grandad likes everyone. He's lovely!"

"I know Mum he is so nice to me."

"He is nice to everyone, son."

"Mum, tell me some Great Gran, Jewish stories, and then I might understand more about what Jewish is."

Chapter #4 *Escape to Sanity*

"Alright, let me tell you what I know about Great Gran and her family, but let's get another cup of tea first."

"Henry, why would you consider taking your family to England? They hate Germans and they hate the Jews. You, comrade, are a German Jew!"

Henry smiled at him, "You, my opinionated friend, have a unique skill at stating the obvious. I'm tired of seeing the fear in my wife's face every time I hear about another pogrom against us Jews. I want to live in a country where a Jew can be the Prime Minister, not just once but twice. That's exactly why I want to take my girls to live in England."

"You want to go to England because Benjamin Disraeli was elected Prime Minister of England? You know he was baptized an Anglican at twelve."

"He was born a Jew and will always be a Jew and made no secret of it and still he became Prime Minister of a great nation. I'm taking my girls to England and safety, there's no telling how bad these pogroms are going to get." Henry said it with such conviction that his friend never spoke of it again.

Eastern Europe and Germany were making it very difficult for Jews in the late 1800's, Henry, Greta and their little girl Mary were bound for England and the good life. Perhaps it wasn't perfect for Jews, but it was far better than Stettin, which was a German port city that was rough, overrun with all manner of sailors and other poor souls that were brought to this city on boats from all over the world. Henry wanted his two girls out of this city and country. He was sure that England was to be the safest place for them. America, it was said was a very safe haven but he knew not one Jew that lived in America. In England he knew many and they all lived and worked in East London and so would he.

"Where will we live in England, Papa?"

"Your mother and I have booked passage on a brand new ship called the SS Deutschland leaving from right here in Stettin. We will land in Southampton and then take the train to London's East end where there are many clothing factories. This old tailor father of yours will make enough money so that you and your beautiful mother will not have to worry again my beautiful little mouse." Mary always laughed when her father called her his little mouse. She felt loved!

Henry, Greta and little Mary travelled on a cart from their squalid flat to the harbour district with every piece of luggage they had. They boarded the huge ship and noticed it had four funnels which Henry had never seen before. Many ships in the harbour had three funnels but four funnels, he'd never seen. He thought this must be a powerful ship. The SS Deutschland was sailing for New York with a stop in Southampton. As the huge ship made its way out of Stettin harbour it started to vibrate violently and the vibrations made a loud noise that frightened his wife and in particular his little mouse. She cried and clung to him so tightly that he completely forgot about the vibrations and noise and focused totally on calming his little girl. Greta asked him above the din of the vibrations.

"What on earth is that horrible noise?"

Henry tried to calm his wife all the time holding his still crying child and shouted back to her, "I haven't a clue." Later Henry went above decks and asked to speak with someone that looked to be in charge.

"Excuse me," he said "Can you tell me what was that very loud noise and shaking vibrations that we experienced earlier?" He used his hands to illustrate a shaking motion, and then he grabbed his ears to explain the noise in case his use of half Yiddish, half German wasn't clear. The young man frowned with disdain at this Jew asking him for an explanation. He answered in a condescending manner, "It's the four funnels. This is a four-funnel ship which makes it faster than most other ships and just to put you at ease this ship has made the transatlantic crossing faster than any other ship to date. We have taken the Blue Riband award from the British for the first time ever with this four-funnelled ship. You'll get to Southampton in record time and the noise and vibration is a small price to pay for the speed of this vessel!" The young officer went on in an arrogant manner to explain that Henry wasn't the first person to be concerned about the vibrations.

On the second day little Mary made a friend. Hector was older than Mary. He was almost a teenager and most definitely Jewish. He was a sorry lad; he had a condition that made his eyes bulge out of his eye sockets. His eyeballs looked like they were straining constantly. Most of the passengers gave him a wide berth because of his condition. Some mocked him openly, because of his unfortunate condition. Mary thought him a nice boy who spoke softly and kindly to her. She did notice his extremely bulging eyes but decided to overlook his condition on account of his kindness. Rather than dismiss her as older boys did, Hector was very curious about her. He and his family were from Stettin too and were escaping the difficulties for the Jewish people.

Little Mary saw Hector almost every time she went to the upper decks, but then for two days she looked for him but couldn't find him anywhere.

When Mary told her father that she couldn't find Hector, her father changed the subject quickly. Mary's mother noticed and asked him about the boy.

"*What happened to him?*" her mother asked in whispering tone.

"He went over, they told us, that is all I know." What *do you mean he went over? Where is that boy? They threw him over you mean*"...her voice raised in horror and distress.

"Keep your voice down or she'll hear you" said Henry. Mary's mother looked at her daughter through her tears and disgust and then cried out. *"What could have happened to that poor boy? Was he thrown overboard to die, alone and afraid? Why? Because he was Jewish...because of his bulging eyes? Heaven help us,"* Greta trembled with disgust and revulsion as she cried through sobs and heaving shoulders.

"What's the matter Momma? Why are you crying and I heard you say Hector's name. Is he alright?" Her father took her into the passageway away from a still crying almost hysterical mother.

"Come now my little mouse; let's have a stroll and a chat. Your mother is missing her home, that's all!" Mary never saw Hector's bulging eyes again for the rest of the voyage and she noticed that her father never let go of her hand except when they were inside the tiny cabin.

On their arrival in Southampton a young, muscular porter offered to help them and their many pieces of luggage to the train station. He smelled horribly of someone that hadn't bathed for some time but Henry was grateful for the help since he wasn't sure where to go. He soon forgot about the smell. The young man didn't care about them being Jewish; he was focused on the money. Henry couldn't understand a word the young man said nor did the young man understand him but with some hand signals and pointing they both communicated well enough to both get what they wanted. The muscular man was paid and the family and their luggage made it to the train station.

Click, clack, click, and mile after mile the train rocked and rolled down the track. Mary looked out, her face pressed against the dirty glass and thought of Hector's bulging eyes. She knew something terrible happened but was afraid to ask. Hector and his eyes would stay in her memory for her entire life. The countryside all looked the same to her.

"Papa what will it be like in East London, tell me again."

"Oh my little mouse, it will be wonderful. There will be little houses all together in rows and the streets are cobblestones and not dirt. The English people are a polite and caring people. They will welcome us and be happy that Papa will be able to sew and mend their clothes. It will be a nice place to live. We'll have a small garden at the back our house. The English are known for their gardens, so I'm told." Little Mary turned back to the window and watched as the fields and houses went by.

Chapter #5 *Banged up*

"So Jewish means that people come from Germany, Mum?"
"No son it doesn't. It's a religion, and it doesn't matter where you come from. You can be Jewish and come from Germany or you can be Jewish and come from here in East London."

"Am I Jewish?" asked the little blonde boy.

"Well, you are part Jewish I suppose."

"Mum this is so hard to understand, this Jewish business."

"Ok son that's enough trying to understand for now. It's time for bed my boy." He was already tired and ready for bed and so didn't complain at all.

The next day was a school day and as usual Jimmy was tired, in a bad mood and didn't want to get out of bed. His mother badgered him several times and finally he got out of his warm cocoon and got dressed.

He got out of the door with a piece of toast, thick with butter and marmalade. With his coat under his arm and his satchel full of school pencils and some paper, he ambled off down the lane to the school. Mary watched as he walked along slowly. He did not really want to get to school and spied an old tin can in the gutter and proceeded to kick it down the cobblestone laneway, hoping that it would delay the inevitable, getting to school.

She wondered what would become of her little man. Off to her first job at the box factory she went. She knew that he'd let himself in after school and play quietly; he had his own key on a string around his neck. On the odd occasion when he lost or forgot his key one of the neighbours would take him in and keep him occupied until her husband got home. Mary worked all day and then caught the bus back home to the pub. She had no sooner put on her pinafore when a neighbour burst through the pub door, out of breath. She tried to tell Mary that the police had come. There was a terrible fight in the street with the police and her boy was screaming. Finally she caught her breath and was able to assure Mary that young Jimmy was with her kids in her house next door to Mary's, but that the police had taken her man away.

Mary ran as fast as her legs would carry her. She was completely out of breath by the time she reached the house and thought to herself *those bleeding fags are killing me I need to stop smoking*. The house was empty and then she realized that her little Jimmy was next door. She tapped on the brass knocker and her neighbour came to the door.

Jimmy heard her voice and he came running and shouted, "Mum, they took him away. They hit him and pushed him on the ground, put handcuffs on him and pushed him so hard into the van that he hit his face and it was bleeding." The little boy said all of that without taking a breath.

Mary got the phone number for the police station and went around to the red phone box on the corner and called the police. She told them her name and her husband's name and the desk Sergeant knew instantly who she was calling about.

"So you are the poor cow married to that horrible bastard. He's a poor excuse for a husband," he said with a very sharp delivery. "We've been after him for many years and we've finally caught him red-handed, thieving was he and he is going inside for a long time my dear so you'd better get used to being apart." She started to cry.

The Sergeant without missing a beat said, "That's enough tears. You must have known you were married to a tea leaf (thief). He never worked but always had money. You are either stupid or you were in on it. Either way I've no sympathy for you young lady." Mary was too shocked to answer. She just quietly hung up the phone and went home and made a fried egg sandwich and a cup of tea and sat looking off into space, not knowing what she'd do. Her young son came into the room and asked if she would tell a few stories tonight. "No, not tonight Jimmy, I'm not in a very good mood." He understood and sat on the arm of the chair and leaned into his mother and put his arms around her neck as she began to cry very quietly.

In the days that followed she was allowed to visit her husband in the Wormwood Scrubs jail. He was sullen and wasn't pleased at all to see her. He was embarrassed and he noticed many of the other inmates ogled her. He was angry with them but took it out on Mary.

"What did you come 'ere for?"

"To see if you are alright, to see if you need anything?"

"I need to get out of this place, that's all. If you can do something to get me out of here, that would be good, but you can't, can you? So, what did you come 'ere for, to see me banged up? Well I'm going to be in 'ere for a long bleeding time and you are going to be on your own, so you'd better get used to it!" She hung her head and looked down. She could not believe that he was being nasty to her even though she'd traveled across London taking 3 different buses to get to Wormwood Scrubs Prison to see him.

She got up and from somewhere a whistle came across the room from an admiring prisoner and she turned beet red with embarrassment and leaned over to kiss him goodbye and he jerked away from her and said in a poisonous manner, "If you ever walk out with another bloke you'll be a bad smell in the cellar or they'll find you floating in the canal." She jerked upright and walked toward the exit without any further conversation with her husband. She caught the same three buses back to her row house and did what all the English do in times of stress; she made a cup of tea!

She needed both of her jobs now just to keep the house going. It was council housing but even the Government wanted their rent money.

Chapter #6 *a rainy night*

A few days after the prison visit things seemed to settle down. Most people on Fish Island in East London knew about the up-coming long prison term and wondered what took the coppers so long to get him. It seemed like the police were the very last to know what the rest of the community had known for so long. He was thieving and hurting people if he had too. He had been most of his working life. Most of the men that lived in East London's Fish Island were either involved directly or indirectly in dodgy gear. They either stole or sold the stuff or provided protection for the people stealing or selling. Almost everyone was earning money from the massive underground economy commonly known as 'The Fiddle'. Fish Island was literally awash in black market merchandise. It was part of the culture so much so that no one really thought of it as illegal, rather just a way to get the goods that everyone needed at a price that the working poor could afford.

"Mum, now that we've had dinner can we have a cup of tea and a story? How did Granddad meet my Jewish Great Gran?"

"It's complicated my boy. You see Great Gran had a baby when she met Great Granddad. She had married a Jewish man just as her Mum and Dad wanted her too. His name was Rosen and he was lost during the first war."

"How did he get lost?"

"No son, he died in France in the 1st war against the Germans."

"Then she married Great granddad?"

"Yes".

"How did they meet each other."

"Well after Great Gran's husband died she wanted to help other soldiers. She volunteered at a local dance hall, where soldiers went while they were having a rest from the war back in England.

***

"Oye, Sarge, come to the Shangri-La with me and see if that 'bit of fluff' is there tonight. She was a bleedin' vision. Honestly, she was the best looking gal I've ever seen in my entire life. No exaggerating Sarge!"

"First off, if she was a vision, she'd have nothing to do with a broken down old squaddie like you Albert. Then secondly what would a real vision be doing at the Shangri-La? Looking for a husband I suspect. You and I both know how most of those women get a man, one night of passion and a life-time looking after screaming, snotty nose kids. Not for me lad. When I'm finished with army life I'll be going back to the lush lands of my forefathers and I'll be buying a plot of land ample enough to raise Scotland's most beautiful horses, not snotty nose kids!"

"Sarge, c'mon, just come with me and see this woman. She has long dark, hair and eyes that looked straight into your soul."

"How would you know if you haven't had the courage to speak with her?"

"Yes but you would. Please Sarge you ain't afraid of anything!"

"Alright, alright!"

******

"Let me buy you a pint Sarge, it's the least I can do for you."

"Lovely, cheers."

"There she is!"

"Ok, keep your hair on, where?"

"Over there by the back door." Yeoman paused as he took a long look and then found himself staring at her. It was as though everything else became a blur and all he saw was her. "Bloody hell you weren't exaggerating this time Albert. She is a vision."

"Sarge, go over and ask her if we can buy her a drink before someone else beats us to it."

"Hello. My name is James, James Yeoman and my corporal and I would like to buy you a drink."

"Does it take two of you to buy a lady a drink? No, thank you, I don't drink."

He stumbled a little, but never took his eyes off her. "Well, what about a pineapple juice?" asked the normally unflappable man from Scotland.

"Look, I've come here to dance with lonely **Jewish** soldiers, and that is all I've come here for. Yes, I'm a Jewess, so off you go and find yourself a gentile girl to buy a drink." She walked away and left the Sergeant and his corporal standing there with their mouths open. Mary spent the next two hours dancing with and chatting to Jewish soldiers just back from the Great War. They always wanted more, to see her again or offered to take her out but Mary had a strict rule, no more soldiers in her life since she had lost her husband to this insanity called war. She put in two good hours dancing and chatting and then grabbed her woollen coat and scarf and headed out to a rainy, drizzling night to walk home. As she left the dance hall a voice broke the evening silence and it unnerved her.

"Let me see you home safely." It was that annoying gentile with the red hair.

"No you can't see me home, and look at you, you are completely soaking all the way through to your skin. How long have you been out here waiting?"

"Since you walked away from me inside and I'm going to tell you something else. I'm going to marry you."

She was so shocked at that pronouncement that she giggled and stepped back to have a better look at this fellow. He was dripping water from every part of his uniform and head and hands. It was running off his nose like a small waterfall.

She laughed again and said, "Alright if it will get you back to your barracks before you catch pneumonia, you can see me home."

"I am going to marry you," he said. "Don't be completely silly man. I don't even know you. You are a soldier, and I've already lost a soldier husband to the bloody war. There won't be a second. Then to top it off you're a gentile. I'm Jewish and I have a two-year old son."

"I don't care if you have 15 children. I'm going to marry you so you might as well come to grips with it." She giggled again and smiled at his insistence on the impossible.

"Papa, mother, please bring some towels. I've rescued a drowning mongrel," she said in English. Then a small stooped-over man appeared with small round spectacles balanced precariously on the end of his nose. He said something in Yiddish and ran to a cupboard for some clothes to help the solider standing dripping water in his front passageway.

"I can make my way back to the barracks. I'll be alright."

"No you can't. At least not until you've dried off a little and had a warm cup of tea." The old bespectacled man appeared in a flash with towels and a rather round, older lady shuffled into the scullery to put the kettle on the boil after another exchange of Yiddish.

"Where's your little boy?" asked the Sergeant. "It is half past ten at night. Where do you think he is? In bed soundly sleeping I hope." Her father nodded in the affirmative. Although he wasn't comfortable speaking English he understood every word.

After he dried off somewhat and drank his hot tea, he stood at the door not wanting to leave there. She handed him a large black umbrella with a yellow cane handle and said, "This is my father's only umbrella. I expect you to bring it back," and she smiled at James for first time. He realized that she would see him again and he never felt like that before in his entire life. He felt like his feet never touched the ground on the long and rainy walk back to the barracks. He was smitten.

****

"Mum, I love that story of Gran and Granddad meeting each other."

"I do too, son. Now off to bed with you, or you are not going to get up for school in the morning."

"Yes I will."

"You always say that but in the morning you want to snuggle down and I have to call you ten times." He walked reluctantly towards his bedroom and soon the numbness of sleep overcame him.

Mary was getting used to living without her husband and somehow, she was managing to keep things afloat financially. Neighbours and friends kept watch over young Jimmy and she managed the trip to the prison every month. Each trip was as fruitless as the last; her husband never seemed grateful to see her and could care less of about the complexity of the trip and the time it took to make that awkward journey to visit him. She was sure he didn't love her, at least he didn't show it in the way her uncles and aunts showed love to each other, but he was a safe port in the storm of her surprise pregnancy at 17. Her older sister had told her to go and pay the £2 to the old lady in Bethnal Green Road and she and her knitting needles would take care of her problem. She had cried at the thought of it but in moments of choking fear and in the quiet of her heart she considered it if only for a moment. Whether it was God or goodness she didn't know, she only knew that if it meant her very life she couldn't do it!

The first question out of his mouth on those visits was, "Did you bring me fags?" Never a smile or a nice warm hello, his eyes never really looked at her in a warm way. She looked at his eyes but his were darting about the visiting area making sure that none of other inmates were ogling her. He never once asked her about the boy, not once. She wondered if this marriage would ever be a real one like that of the home she grew up in with her Jewish grandmother and Scottish grandfather. Her Granddad was forever telling her Gran that he loved her and was touching her. Even at their advanced years he'd steal a kiss on the cheek and she'd tell him not to be so silly in front of the grandkids but young Mary knew that secretly her Gran loved it.

This Scottish father and Jewish mother had seven children as well as the boy that she brought into the marriage. James treated the boy no different than his own seven.

Rich was the son with the Jewish last name. Georgie was the oldest child born of their love. Then came Jim, a mild-mannered reader who had an insatiable appetite for knowledge, the more technical the better. His two older brothers teased him for his unusual ability to process complicated technical instruction and information. Dora, the oldest girl, a red-head with a temper to match, was a slight, trim girl, pretty but with a strong and forceful spirit about her which attracted most men much to her husband's annoyance. Her husband's name was Richard but everyone called him Dick. He kept saying his name was Richard but still everyone called him Dick. He wanted so much to be a 'Richard' because it sounded more upscale but he came from working class people and much to his constant irritation he was 'Dick'. Dick was from the docklands of Liverpool, which automatically made him a character. He always had a story especially of his days in the merchant navy as a ship's cook in WW2. His favorite story was when he managed to steal and smuggle meat that was rationed because of the war. "Did I tell you the time that we docked at the Royal Victoria dock in Canningtown? I managed to 'appropriate' two ten pound tins; one tin of corned beef and one of ham. I got to the police stationed at the dock gate with all this grub in my duffle bag and the police said, "Well young man, anything to report."

"I said in a sarcastic fashion. Yes I've got twenty pounds of meat in my bloody duffle bag." The two police looked at each other and said, "Go on, on your way you cheeky beggar."

"Little did they know that's exactly what I did have in my gear and they laughed at me and let me walk straight through? I dodged a bullet that day. Aye, if they would have searched my belongings, I would have ended up in the brig for a month for stealing. In the end the family had lots of meat which was so scarce because of the rationing during the war." That was his favorite story and he loved the telling of it, but on the odd occasion he'd tell another story. Sometimes he'd hold back tears, or choke as words and breaths got mixed up in the emotion of the retelling. As a merchant seaman he was in the North Atlantic on a convoy, where ships were blown up by German submarines and the sailors that survived the explosions were bobbing up and down in the rough seas cheering on the convoy knowing that they couldn't stop to pick them up since that would cause them to be sitting ducks for the U-boats. They would die, some from drowning, others quietly but painfully from hypothermia, but still they cheered on their comrades in arms that had made it through the gauntlet of underwater missiles.

Dora, the oldest of the Yeoman girls was an office worker at one of the big factories on the north side of the Thames. They made cables and wires that were used in all manner of big engineering projects. After the 2nd World War Dick left the merchant navy and he worked as a labourer in the same factory except he worked the night shift while Dora was a 9 to 5er. They didn't make much more than minimum wages but always managed to slip a few schillings a week in her Mum's handbag.

The front door at 173 Herbert Road opened and closed and then came the unmistakable cadence of Lily's footsteps. She was the 2nd girl born to James and Mary. Lily was born a perfect little girl but for a club foot that didn't seem important when she was a baby but it became obvious that without medical help this child would not walk. So, started a series of operations and painful braces that worked to strengthen and straighten the offending foot and while the effect was successful in as much as Lily was able to walk she had to wear shoes that offered her club foot a sole that was a few inches higher since the deformity made her club foot much shorter. This combination of a shorter leg and the club foot gave her an odd leaning type cadence as she walked. What Lily lacked in mobile abilities she more than made up for in tenacity and grit. Lily was afraid of nothing, not man nor beast. People would feel sorry for her and her club foot and her funny walk until they met her, then the empathetic feeling would turn into awe at this fearless handicapped girl. It was thought she'd have trouble finding a husband but nothing could have been further from the truth. One day she came home with a small man who had extremely large teeth that didn't seem to belong in his mouth and the offending teeth seemed to get in the way when he spoke, which he didn't do often. Lily announced to her mother and father in the living room at 173 Herbert Road, that Sidney and she were to be married. James and Mary liked Sidney right away. They asked him a few questions about himself and when they did he looked to Lily and she'd answer on his behalf. This happened every time they appeared together at the house. In the end the old couple wondered if he could speak at all. It turned out he could, he just wanted to get it right for Lily, and no one knew if it was for the love or fear of her.

Eva, the middle girl was not bright like her two older sisters but instead possessed a loving, unbridled, simple kindness that made her popular with neighbours and family. Eva had an unquenchable sweet tooth and was never found too far away from anything sweet. Any money she got her hands on growing up was spent at the corner sweet shop. Even as she married and had children her penchant for sweets seemed to consume all of her waking moments. It caused grief between her and her husband, Jock, a short, rugged faced man from the Scottish city of Glasgow. Jock was very frugal with money and food to the point that it bordered on abusive behaviour but Eva was oblivious to the fact. She was blindly and hopelessly in love with Jock. The rest of the family tolerated him but only for family peace and because James and Mary insisted on it. Anything thing this couple asked of their family was never questioned.

Chris was the baby girl of the family, cared for and watched over by her big sisters. Whether that helped to form her character was unclear but Chris wasn't able think for herself. All her opinions and information was from her mother, father and most importantly of all her sisters. This tribe of sisters carried and fetched for her, would speak for her and provide all of her physical and emotional needs. As she grew into a woman it seemed to take away her ability to reason for herself or develop values and principles that were of her own making. She married a man from the Herefordshire, a farm labourer who was so domineering and hard, he made every decision for Chris to the point that she became invisible in the relationship and in life itself. The sisters hated him and the feeling was reciprocated with an even higher degree of visceral emotion.

Maud was the middle girl and the unabashed favourite child of Mary and James. She was the gold standard by which every other child was measured and everyone knew it. Maud was devoted to the family, loved her mother but she worshipped her father. When James walked into the room Maud's face would erupt in smiling. She loved to sit with him and be close to him. She hung on every word and her favourite thing was to look at his face as it seemed to be her safe place. Mary watched this emotional connection between her husband and daughter over the years and would lovingly roll her eyes at this love kinship, but in reality she was in awe of it. Secretly she worried what would become of this girl if/when anything happened to her man, but put it out of her mind. It was too painful to contemplate.

Chapter #7 *Stark Fear*

Mary didn't need a social life. She had one of sorts working three nights a week in the pub. Many boys and some men flirted with her. Some even asked her out on a date despite the obvious wedding ring prominently displayed on her left hand. That was until they learned who she was married to and what he would do to them if it got back to him that anyone was trying to blag his woman. He was feared, even though he was banged up. He could still have someone give a bloke a good hiding or worse. So most of the local talent, while nice to her, were never really serious about pressing the issue for fear of the result of their misadventure.

Her life was days at the box factory, evenings at the pub and then home to little Jimmy who was almost always asleep in front of the telly. Sometimes she'd think of her sister's advice and her stomach would tighten and grip her like a vice and quickly she'd put that thought out of her mind. In a way she hated her sister for putting even the thought of that nightmare in her conscious mind. She loved this little blond boy; he was the only thing of real goodness in her miserable married life. She still felt like a little girl only with a son of her own.

"I thought you might be happy to see me," she said to her inmate husband on a visit to the Wormwood Scrubs jail.

"Listen carefully woman. Next Tuesday a delivery is going to arrive at our gaff. Don't ask any questions or tell anyone. Just keep quiet and wait for the word on when that delivery will be picked up."

"What are you talking about, what kind of delivery?"

"You stupid cow, I just told you not to ask bleedin' questions. Just shut up and do as you're told or that boy of yours will not just be a bastard; he'll an orphan as well."

She started to shake and tremble from fear of what she was getting involved in. She was holding a cigarette and she started to shake so uncontrollably that the ash and burning tobacco were falling onto her lap.

"Get a hold of yourself woman. If you can't control yourself better than this we'll be caught and you'll be in a woman's prison." That sent her to another level of fear and she started to sob uncontrollably. The slap came fast and hard across her face; it was to shock her out of her overwhelming fear. All of the heads turned towards the sound of the blow. Two burly prison guards raced to the spot and grabbed him and held him down until three additional guards appeared and struggled to contain him.

His eyes bulged out of his head and he screamed at her, "Do as I told you, you stupid cow, or else." She got up, ran out of the meeting hall and made her way through the hallways, locked doors and finally out of the prison itself. She gasped and opened her mouth as fully as she could and sucked in all the air she could take in again and again. She just wanted to breathe fresh clean air, as if it would clean out all the mess her life had become marrying that man and settling for profound unhappiness and thinking it couldn't get any worse. She was now to be involved in a crime that could land her who knows where.

No was the word that came to her mind…and then she said it out loud…No…quietly…then she said it loudly…NO!

On the long ride back to Fish Island, her small row house and her boy, Mary's mind wandered. *Why did my Dad have to die at 36? He was so tough and strong. Why did his heart give out at such a young age? Why did he leave me to live with Gran and Granddad? How did I come to get pregnant and marry this…this criminal. If my Dad was alive he'd deal with this man and what he is asking me to do, he'd protect me.* She racked her brain for an answer…and in the end only one came. *She'd run as far away as fast as she could. Her mind wandered back to her dead father.*

Chapter #8 *Awash in Shoes*

Georgie Yeoman was a good father or at least as good as he could be under the circumstances. He provided for his kids, all of them. He and his wife had four girls and one boy who was the oldest. He was only the oldest since the first boy born, Bobby, died in his sleep when he was only a few months old. The doctor said it wasn't uncommon in those squalid old flats with no heating except the fireplace in the front room. The heat never made it back to the bedrooms and the rising damp was everywhere, so on a cold November morning he left them....no crying, no pomp or ceremony he just evaporated from their squalid flat and their squalid lives and left them to ponder why, but only in their minds. It became unseemly to mention his name or what happened. She wondered if Georgie secretly blamed her for their loss. She wasn't much of a mother; she loved her ale too much. She wanted to be at the pub with the noise, lights and other men who flirted with her and bought her ale...they both knew that mothering wasn't natural for her.

Georgie was from a good home, one that spoke of God, Jewish and otherwise and servitude to others. His Scottish father and Jewish mother had raised him right but he had fallen in with the wrong crowd. The thieving and criminality seemed like an easy way of making good money without work and then she trapped him the way many woman trap men. And he quietly succumbed to his life on the gray side of society. His mother and father lived in quiet hope that he'd instill some of the values they taught him his whole life to his children but he couldn't with her living in the house with the kids. She was base and bawdy and most of the kids had turned out the same except one, little Mary. She had spent much of her growing years with Georgie's Jewish mother and Scottish father...she was different! He thought he was going to lose that little girl the same way he lost his first born when he woke and found her blue with cold and crying from hunger. Her mother was still in bed sleeping off a skin full of ale. He took her to his mother and father and said, "You'd better look after this one or we'll find her dead one frosty morning like her brother." They didn't put up a fuss and took the little one. Her mother never asked about her, she knew better.

On Fish Island and in all of the London's East End there were hard men and then there were hard men without a conscience. Those were the dangerous ones. They didn't care if they were caught or worse they didn't care what they needed to do to make sure they didn't get caught. Georgie wasn't one of them. He was hard to be sure, and he was five foot nine and built like a brick bunker, much like his Scottish father. He started out as a minder, protecting anyone that would pay him. He'd take on anyone; men much taller and heavier would fall to him. No one could knock him off his feet. He took a punch like a brick wall and when he landed one of his own the recipient usually went down, if not the first blow then certainly the second. As his legend grew he was in more and more demand, but 'minding' only gave him chump change. He wanted the real money which was in the thieving. So Georgie finally graduated from 'minding' to 'the Rob'. The same quick, hardness that made him a feared street fighter came in handy during the robberies and he soon learned to deal with the fences that bought the stolen merchandise. In the early years they took advantage of him but not for long. He quickly caught on and soon was getting the hang of 'the Rob' and how to maximize the profit from it.

Georgie and his crew were tipped off to a small East London warehouse holding twelve hundred pairs of women's shoes which had been transported from Japan via

South Hampton, to be distributed all over the north of England. They swooped in at two in the morning with crowbars and a large nondescript van. The company that had imported the shoes had a sixty-seven-year old night watchman in the warehouse.

Georgie grabbed the old night watchman by the arm and said, "I'm 'ere for those shoes mate."

"Gov'ner I'm not big enough or stupid enough to try to stop you." Georgie grabbed the old man and slid a ten pound note in his palm. "I'm 'aving this merchandize with your 'elp or without it but I don't want you to get into trouble. So I'm going to tie you up and put you in the office. You'll have this tenner for your troubles and none of my men will harm you in anyway…you have my word!" The old man went off without hesitation and sat in the boss' chair. They tied him to the chair and he swivelled around and around. Then in an act of defiance toward his employer he chuckled as he put his feet up on the desk and smiled at his good fortune, a month's wages. And he was treated well by the thieves. He almost admired them.

****

"Georgie, I'm sorry mate, you can't store that gear 'ere son."

"You told me I could!" replied a panic-stricken Georgie Yeoman.

"The owner of the warehouse has decided to pay a visit this week and he'll see the stuff and know that I'm involved in receiving stolen merchandise. I can't do it lad, I just can't, I'd lose me job and be nicked by the 'old bill'. Naw, sorry Georgie but you'll have to find another gaff to store this stuff until you can move it out!" Sweat started to form on Georgie's brow as he was driving around in the middle of the night with twelve hundred pairs of ladies' shoes worth hundreds of pounds in a borrowed van. *I'll have to put them in my own gaff that's all there is to it* thought Georgie. He pulled up outside his small two-bedroom flat and let himself in. He woke up his woman and kids and at four am they and the crew carried twelve hundred pairs of fancy women's shoes up a flight of stairs into the top flat of the two up, two down maisonette. "Oye you lot, do not make any noise or I'll cuff you round the earhole. Just carry as many boxes of shoes as you can up the stairs." It took hours and they finished just as the sun was coming up over the factory roofs. The crew was paid off. They all received a ten pound note for one night's work of breaking into the warehouse, loading a van, tying up an old night watchman and then taking the loot to Georgie's flat. They did all this before the sun came up. One last job to do was to take back the borrowed van. He left a five pound note on the seat, wrapped around a bottle of good scotch for his mate that lent him the van. He walked back to the flat, walked slowly up the stairs and was met by a sea of shoe boxes. Everywhere he looked he saw boxes. In the bedrooms they were piled floor to ceiling, in every nook a cranny and under beds. He wasn't even able to close the toilet door behind himself because of the boxes. He sat down in his favourite chair exhausted, put his feet up on several boxes of ladies shoes and started to laugh. Georgie put his head back on the chair and went soundly to sleep…it had been a long night's work!

****

"Mum, mum I wished I could be like your Dad, big and strong and fearless."

"Do you think I could grow up to be like him?"

"I don't think so darling. You are a bit different than your Granddad. You're more like your Great Granddad."

"Please tell me more stories about your dad. Do you have any more stories about him?"

"Well my dad was a bit of a mystery. He made his living in a different way."

"What do you mean Mum?"

"He was a minder. He took care of people that were in danger or afraid and they would pay him."

"Why were they afraid? What were they afraid of?"

"Well some people get into trouble or make people upset and they might want to hurt them. Your Granddad would make sure that they never got hurt."

"You mean like the time John Young at #6 said he was going to thump me and I was afraid."

"Yes, that's right. Your granddad would have protected you from the boy at #6 and if you had money you would have paid him for doing that favour for you." "Oh, I see he must have been very brave." With that statement his young mother broke down and sobbed. Jimmy realized he'd asked too many questions with painful consequences for his Mum. After a few minutes she said, "Let me tell you how strong and brave your Granddad was..."

Bang, bang, bang, bang, bang on the door knocker at number 12 Monier Road, sounded like a machine gun on Fish Island in London East End on a quiet Sunday morning. "Who's that banging on the door at this time on a Sunday morning? Blimey someone is excited and in a bleedin' hurry! Georgie, Georgie, hurry up. Come down the stairs."

"Is he ere? Get your old man down 'ere...now!"

"I'm putting my trousers on. Wait a bloody minute. Who is it?"

Georgie almost fell down the flight of stairs that were covered in a cheap carpet worn threadbare, the stairs that led straight onto the street. When he awkwardly got to the street level there were two men.

"You the bastard that stole our gear away the other night?" And the bigger of the two men reached into the doorway obviously trying to reach Georgie Yeoman. He grabbed his shirt and went to pull Georgie out of the doorway of his home. He didn't get a chance to as the hunted was not planning to be the hunted. Instinct took over and all five-foot nine of him lunged at the bigger of the two men with speed and the single purpose of mind to knock him down. All the years of being a 'minder' of people that needed protecting and his natural need to survive by whatever force he could muster took over. He landed a punch and as he did he felt something snap. He wondered for a split second was it his hand or fingers. It sounded like a crack and a thud at the same time. The bigger of the two thugs went down with the one punch. Both men standing looked at the body lying on the ground convulsing and then at once it became obvious that his bladder had let go. He was urinating and convulsing at the same time. He was oblivious to it all; he had been knocked out with one blinding hammer-like blow. Georgie broke his gaze at the man on the ground and looked menacingly at his next victim, the one who had insulted his wife, banged very loudly on Yeoman's door this Sunday morning and woke up the entire neighborhood with his threatening language. Georgie reached and grabbed his collar and the man went to his knees and put his hands up pleading, "I'm sorry mate, I didn't realize who you were. We were paid to mind the gaff where gear was being stored and it went missing the night before last. Our Gov'ner said he knew it was the bloke who lives at 12

Monier Road but if I'd known it was Georgie Yeoman, I'd never have come 'ere. I'm sorry. Let me go so I can take care of my mate. I think he's really in a bad way."

Georgie slapped him hard at the back of his head but held him in place at arm's length with a hold like that of a vice grip.

"You go back to your Gov'ner and tell him that he needn't send anyone to my house with my family here again or I'll be coming to his house and I'll drag him out of his house and beat the living shit out of him in front of his wife and kids...got it? Make sure you tell him in plain language so he won't be confused." He shook the man like one shakes a dusty mat and then released him. He fell to the ground and leaned over his friend who was starting to come around. The small man helped his friend get to his feet and the two made an uncourageous retreat looking over their shoulders. A neighbour from two doors away watched from the safety of his doorway and Georgie still high from the adrenalin caught him staring.

Georgie growled, "What are you looking at?" The door slammed shut very fast.

They closed the door and made their way up the stairs to the flat. Dolly complained to George. "I asked you not to bring the shoes 'ere."

"Dolly I told you if I 'ad somewhere else to take the gear I would have. Now let's get upstairs and let's hope that no one sent for the law. If the old bill comes round 'ere I'm done for, well and truly. I've got to find a way to flog these bleedin' shoes without you nagging me." Dolly made her way up the steep, worn stairs and lit a cigarette to calm her nerves. She was trembling so hard, she had difficulties lighting the cigarette. She stood for a minute and took several deep draws on the cigarette. She felt the smoke fill her lungs but her hands were still shaking. Dolly remembered the beer still in the sideboard from last night and was tempted, but she thought better of it and instead put the kettle on the boil for a cup of tea instead. The coppers never came that day and Georgie knew that as night fell he needed to move the stolen merchandise and did. His four daughters and his son were all as coarse and mean as the streets that they were brought up in, except for the oldest girl raised from a baby by her grandparents until she was in her teens. She was a compliant child that was in awe of her father and afraid of her mother. Her name was Mary, named after her Jewish grandmother.

It was a Monday morning when the kids were getting ready to start the day. Mary was fourteen and in her last year at school. Her older brother, George junior, who was sixteen had finished school and had taken a job as a laborer. He was tall, maybe six foot one unlike his five foot nine father and he fancied himself a bit of a tough bloke but in truth he wasn't. He knew who and what his old man was and he desperately wanted to be that hard, but didn't have it in him and what was worse, he knew it! They were finishing breakfast or at least a poor excuse for breakfast of cold strong tea and burnt toast dripping with butter when it dawned on them that their dad wasn't sitting in his chair smoking a Senior Service cigarette and reading the Daily Mirror. "Your far'ver is still in bed." The words stopped short as though she almost thought she should say more but didn't. The two oldest kids looked at each other in disbelief. They had never actually seen their father in his bed at any time in their young lives.

"'E's feeling a little dickey, been up all night," grunted Dolly between hard draws on her unfiltered Senior Service cigarette. Some loose tobacco had got between her teeth and she spit it onto the worn linoleum in the small cold scullery of a kitchen.

Later that day Mary was called to the head master's office and was told she should go straight home as soon as possible. Dread washed over her. At that very moment she knew something was very wrong. When she reached the street she looked and saw many people, mostly women with their hair in curlers wrapped in scarves standing around the doorway of her flat. Her stomach tightened as an unknown fear gripped her. As she reached the doorway to the stairs that lead to the upstairs flat that was her home, the people looked at her and never said a word but parted. She ran between them up the stairs but she didn't want to reach the top. Her mother Dolly sat in 'his' chair sobbing and smoking all at the same time.

Mary spoke in her small and fearful voice hesitantly, "What's the matter Mum?"

"'E's dead, your bleedin' far'ver is dead," and with that she convulsed so hard that it frightened little Mary that her Mum might not be able to breathe. A neighbour came alongside of her and put her hand on Dolly's shoulder which seemed to settle her down to a quiet sobbing. Mary moved toward the door of her parent's bedroom. She couldn't process the facts that she'd just been given and stood there not knowing whether she should go in. Could she handle seeing her hero lying still and dead. The same neighbour reached out and said, "Lovie you don't want to see your daddy like this. Just remember him as he was…darlin'…alright?"

Mary just stood there for the longest time, frozen somehow, not knowing what to do. She was desperate to see him one last time but didn't know what happened to dead people. She wondered what he would look like, the uncertainty of the moment made her want to run away, but where would she go. Instead she evaporated to her room and cried into her pillow. It wasn't the last time she would see him. Two days later an open casket was placed in the small living room and people came to say goodbye to Georgie Yeoman. Mary didn't like the way her dad looked. He was an odd colour, but he did look nice in his best suit and white shirt and royal blue tie. It was a like a circus, so many people tried to get in. Georgie was a local legend, and even those that feared him came to pay their respects. People filled the small living room and had to turn sideways to get past the open casket into the small kitchen for another glass of brown ale or a cup of strong, warm tea. "Dolly, Dolly, come 'ere quick!" shouted an old friend.

Dolly went down the stairs and standing in the crowd was the local Sergeant of the police from Bow Street station. He said, "Your Georgie was a villain there's no doubt, but he was fair and never let any old girl or kid go without. He even helped a few of our lot from time to time. My inspector would have my guts for garters if he knew I'd come 'ere today but I had to pay my respects to your old man. Even though we all wanted to put him away, we had a grudging respect for him Dolly." With that the new widow broke down and sobbed, and the police Sergeant made a discreet withdrawal. The old Scottish father and Jewish mother didn't make the trip to the funeral. They said goodbye to their son in their hearts since they were at odds with his choice of a wife. They stayed on the south side of the river Thames, where they had spent the past thirty years. The doctors reported that their Georgie died of a heart valve defect and in the end his heart failed. He was only thirty-six and strong as an ox with a neck that seemed too big for the head that it carried. Their Georgie was gone, the first child of their love for each other. That was not lost on both of them. Old James Yeoman had lost so many over the years. He had endured the Boer war followed by the Great War, but nothing was as devastating as the loss of his Georgie.

****

Tonight's story about her father made him cry but he didn't know why. Perhaps it was her loss that he felt for the first time and it moved the little boy to tears.

After the story and several warm sweet cups of tea, Mary said to her son, "Jimmy we have to leave here."

Jimmy asked, "Why Mum, where are we going?"

"I don't know."

"What about school?"

"I don't know Jimmy. Stop asking me questions that I can't answer. My mind is in a spin."

"Why are we leaving at night Mum. I'm starting to get scared. You seem frantic."

"I'm sorry son. I am really sorry but you'll just have to trust me. We have got to leave this house tonight." She had nobody she could trust on this side of the river Thames. Her sisters and brother were estranged from her. Her father was long since dead and she had to get away from this husband that was planning to have her involved in a criminal activity from his jail cell. She'd met some of his so-called business associates. They scared her, and they were the type with no conscience, hard frightening men. She knew that her safety and perhaps her very life was really at risk.

Chapter #9 *Fear had found her*

Months had gone by and the arrival of Mary and her boy Jimmy was sometimes a joy to the old couple and sometimes when James whined too much or was naughty the old fellow chaffed at having his granddaughter and great grandson living with them.

"Why are we living here with nanny and granddad, why can't we go home to our own house Mum?"

"It's not safe my love, Nanny and Granddad are letting us stay here."

"How long will we have to stay here?"

"I don't know, please don't ask again."

****

"I love the market on Saturday morning, my love; the smells and the sounds of people buying and selling, it's like a pleasant thing to me but I'm not sure why."

"You soppy old sweetheart, you like everything. It's just the dirty, noisy old Woolwich market."

"Come on let's treat ourselves to a nice cup of tea," said his aging wife. Just then a man, fifty years his junior grabbed his arm and said, "Where is she old man?"

"I beg your pardon."

"Let go of my husband!" shouted Mary. "Shut up you old fat Jewish cow." Something snapped in old James, despite his seven decades of life. He instinctively grabbed the man by the throat with one hand and with one fluid bulldozer-like motion pushed the man between two stalls that sold fruits and vegetables, and up on the sidewalk against a brick building. The younger man was trying to catch his breath and desperately trying to release himself from the unrelenting grip that this seemly nice old unassuming man had him in, but he wasn't able to.

"I believe you owe my wife an apology, young man," said James in a quiet but deliberate fashion. With no hesitation he squeezed the thug's throat a little harder to make his point and he got a "yes" from the young man's eyes. All at once James realized that people had started to gather around him and so he released his grip and the assailant fell to the ground like a collapsed suit of clothing.

"I was sent to find her. She is to go 'ome, or else."

"Or else what? My wife is still waiting for that apology." James took a half step toward the man still sitting on the pavement trying to pull himself together and rubbing his throat. "I'm sorry missus that I called you names."

"Who sent you with the message?"

"I can't say, all I was told was tell her to go back 'ome or else. These blokes are not to be messed with." Mary moved toward James and slid her hand around his arm and whispered, "We should go home." James picked up his two bags of groceries and the big onion that had rolled under the market barrow in the melee and walked toward the bus stop to get back to 173 Herbert Road, in Plumstead. They didn't talk much on the bus ride home. "I'll put the kettle on lovie. We've had a bit of a shock," said his wife of forty plus years as he sat heavily on a kitchen chair and held his head in his hand. The kitchen or scullery as they still called it, which was an old-fashioned name for what was now called a kitchen. It was sparse and cold unlike the rest of the big house. It was owned by the council, a civic housing project that provided housing for the working poor and since James was unable to find work since leaving the army many years before. The council had provided this four-bedroom home in the south London borough of Plumstead. It had once been the home of a well-to-do family that must have fallen on hard times and the local government took the house for unpaid taxes and then provided it to James and Mary and his large family. They had three boys and five girls who had all grown up at 173 Herbert Road happily and without the visceral knowledge that their father served his country in the Boer war and then in the Great War. After both wars James struggled to adjust to life outside the military. He had reached the level of Sergeant Major and became used to the perks of leadership; men bowing and scraping to his orders. He was a favourite of the commissioned officers and so was treated with dignity and respect from above and below. Then there was life outside the army. He was an ordinary bloke; people didn't care what he was in the army. He was just one of the huddled, unemployed masses that needed a job. James was unable to find meaningful work, but worse and to his profound shame he was unable to keep a job. Mary had realized long ago that something was wrong. Her man, so successful in the army, wasn't able to keep a job as a warehouseman or a night watchman without getting sacked. She knew that his pride wouldn't allow him to take direction from people that he didn't respect or believe had the right, but his wages gave them the right. However his pride wouldn't allow him to assume a subservient position to men that weren't his equal. He and his family were kept by the government by subsidized housing and a small army pension and by money that each of the kids gave to James and Mary, money that both James and Mary knew they could little afford.

Chapter #10 *the Favour*

"Dad, what are we going to do with young Mary and her Jimmy? They can't live with you and Mum forever."

"I know darling, your Mother and I are very concerned for her safety especially after what that bloke at the market said."

"Dad that's all the reason to sort something out for them. What if more of those kinds of blokes come around? Georgie isn't here to deal with them and, forgive me Dad but you're not getting any younger, you know." She touched him on the shoulder as a sign of affection.

He smiled as reassuringly as he could but they both knew she was right. "I've written to an old friend, that owes me a big favour. He lives in the U.S. in the state of Texas, in a town called Boerne. I've called in that favour and asked him to keep Mary and her Jimmy for a time. It would get her out of London and out of harm's way."
"Texas?"

"That is cowboys and rodeos. I can't imagine a little east London girl and her son finding their way in cowboy country, can you Dad?"

"Maudie, I know it's a long way but at least they'll be safe and away from his clutches."

Weeks had passed since the incident in the Woolwich market; it did roll across James mind from time to time. He wondered how they knew he and his wife would have been in the market unless they followed them. Over a cup of tea and his morning Daily Mirror newspaper he realized that they must know where they lived. He felt a small bead of sweat form over his eyebrow as the realization dawned on him that whoever wanted young Mary returned to her matrimonial home knew exactly where she was.

Little Jimmy was frustrated being apart from his school and school chums. He couldn't really understand why he couldn't just go home. "Why are we living here with nanny and granddad? Why can't we go home to our own house Mum?"

"It's not safe my love, Nanny and Granddad are letting us stay here."

"Mum I just want to go home," whined little Jimmy.

****

"Granddad, why would I consider going to a far-off place like Texas. I don't know a soul there."

"I know my darling but you'll be safe there, just think about it. I can't protect you twenty-four hours a day forever. I'm more afraid for you and your boy to stay in London, even though I understand it will be lonely in a new place, in a new country. My friend from Boerne, Texas is prepared to keep you and Jimmy for a while until your husband forgets about you and moves on. Once he gets out of prison he'll be looking for you himself not just sending local thugs to search you out. Then you will truly be in trouble. He is dangerous and unpredictable, plus I'm a little worried for your Nan and me. He has already had one of his people confront us at the Woolwich Market; heaven knows what lengths he'll go to!" Old James was starting to feel guilty at convincing her to run away to the U.S. He knew she loved him and would do almost anything for her beloved granddad. He knew even though it would be very lonely and hard for her, this defensive move, albeit extreme, would keep her safe and so he assuaged the small amount of guilt with that rationalization.

"Can you give me a little time to think about this granddad? I'm afraid to go but I might be even more afraid to stay." He smiled as reassuringly as he could and left the room.

****

"Mum, why would we move to Texas? Do I know anyone there?" he looked at her quizzically and asked. "Where is Texas Mum?" Young Mary smiled at the naiveté of her son, he was trying to sound so knowledgeable and grown up. "Texas is a very far off place that is in America, Jimmy and its cowboy country. Your Great Granddad has a friend that lives there, that wants us to come and stay with them for a while, sort of a long holiday, what do you think?"
"How did Granddad get a friend in that far-off place Mum?"
"We'll have a cup of tea and I'll tell you the story."

Jed Parker lived outside Boerne, Texas on a large land holding that he inherited from his father. It was originally twice the size but after the Great War he and his brother figured it best to split up the land his father had amassed. While his brother raised longhorn cattle, Jed stayed with the Charolaise cattle just like his father had before him. He and his wife Shirley never had children. His brother Jack had two boys named Jim and Jack Jr. Jim was a career soldier, while Jack left the ranch and headed for the bright lights and big city of Dallas. The family only heard from him at Christmas most years or if he got in a jam and needed a few dollars.

Boerne was nestled in the Texas hill country; it was truly a western ranch town, a thirty-minute drive from the city of San Antonio or as the locals called it San Antone.

Jed Parker owed James Yeoman his life or at least he believed he did. Jed was a part of the 1st division of the American Expeditionary Force, who joined the fight in October of 1917. They entered the trenches near Nancy, France. During a raid Jed became disorientated and lost his way and found himself in the British area of the no mans land between the German and British trenches. As he was trying to find his way back, a land mine went off with a blinding flash and a noise that burst both eardrums. He went to the ground and struggled to get up until he realized through the shock that he was bleeding from a gaping shrapnel wound in his left thigh. He was unable to walk and the bleeding was considerable. He was able to crawl to an artillery cart and leaned up against the cart's large wheel. He hoped and prayed that he might see a medic but all he saw was retreating British artillery soldiers trying desperately to get back to the safety of their trenches.

"Hey Buddy can you help me?" shouted Jed but in the frantic, desperate need to reach safety, he was ignored. He shouted again and again, but no one even paused. He tried shouting louder but nothing, they didn't even pause and finally in utter exhaustion and weak from blood loss he gave up. As he fell back in resignation, a short but solid Scotsman that was part of the retreating raid stopped and paused in front of the young American sitting up against the wheel of an artillery cart. James stopped even though his men were screaming at him not to stop, telling him to move with them and to hurry up at it. He stood for a moment and somehow understood that the American was not going anywhere unless someone carried him back to the line. The only issue was that the pair of them would have been a slow and easy target for the chatter of machine gun fire that was unceasing. The two men looked at each other for a split second, the ask was made from the eyes and accepted without words. The young Sergeant Major reached down and grabbed the young American GI and with one fluid movement whipped him over his shoulder in a fireman's carry. The GI screamed with the pain but was grateful to this man he'd never met or knew. He knew what being left behind would have meant and he wanted to live. James took off at a trot. Even with the load on his back he moved quickly and somehow caught up to his band of brothers. They cheered as he lowered the American GI over the trench and then slid himself over into safety, at least for the moment. The doughboy was taken away on a stretcher. A few days later an American Sergeant came looking for James Yeoman and he told him that the man whose life he had saved wanted to thank him personally. Off James went to meet Jed Parker from Boerne, Texas.

"If you had not stopped I would have never seen the Texas hill country again," and then he wept.

James felt compassion for the young man. "Come on lad you would have done the same for me," said James. "No!" answered Jed, "Hundreds of men ran past me but no one stopped. They just gave me fearful looks and kept going. You, James, were the only one to stop. Thank you!" he wept again.

There was a long pause and finally James broke the awkward silence, "You better concentrate on getting better so we can win this bleedin' war and then we can all get 'ome to our families, you to your country and me to mine." Then came the offer, interspersed through emotional sobs, "James, one day you'll need a favour from me and it will be my honour to help you in any way I can."

James just smiled and said, "You get better young man."

"Before you go would you give me your home address, I'd like to keep in touch?"

"Of course," said James. After that interaction James Yeoman took the long walk back to his unit in a drizzling rain and immediately forgot the young American soldier.

In time came the first of many letters, he would receive from a mysterious place called Boerne, Texas. And over the years he wrote a few back. Although James wasn't much of a writer, he just told his wife Mary what to say and she wrote the words for him. Now all these years later the two men had grown old but the favour still remained unused until this request to take in young Mary and her little blonde boy.

Jed jumped at the chance to repay the man for whom he owed his very life. Jed drove into San Antonio, to the US immigration department and told them a lie. He said that his niece from England wanted to spend some time with them on the ranch. It wasn't as difficult as he thought it would be and the papers were completed! All that was needed was a decision by Mary herself.

In the front parlour at 173 Herbert Road, Plumstead, south London with a hearty coal fire spitting and popping in the hearth, James and his aging wife Mary sat with young Mary their granddaughter. They explained that all the arrangements were made and this was her safe passage from the fear and uncertainty that awaited her if she stayed. Mary sobbed uncontrollably as she knew what this meant. The likelihood of seeing either of these two people again was remote and what about the rest of the family. The five sisters that were really her aunts were more like big sisters. She loved them but more and she needed them. She was standing and then the grief of the moment made her legs buckle and she clutched her middle and her grandmother held her but said nothing. There was nothing to say.

Chapter #11 *Texas*

The propeller engine came to life sputtering and popping until it reached its crescendo, and then the other engine followed suit until both engines were at full power and ready for runway #26 at the London airport. Young Mary cried into her hankie and looked out of the window trying to not let her son see her grief. She wondered if she'd ever see England again. It was an unusually sunny and warm London day as they set off. She and her Jimmy took a viscount propeller plane to Gander, Newfoundland, then to New York City, onto Nashville, Tennessee and then finally after twenty-seven hours they landed at the San Antonio airport. It was so hot when she landed, she felt like it would take her breath away. The sun baked down on the pair, mother and child. Jimmy tried to take off his suit jacket but Mary told him to keep it on. She wanted to make a good impression. "Mum I can't keep it on; it's so hot I feel like I'm melting." Jimmy wore a blue tweed suit with dress shorts matching the jacket, long knee socks and dress shoes. His tie and dress shirt were a little wrinkly from the long journey. Jed's hired man drove him into the airport in the 1954 Dodge Regent. It was a two-tone green model, with plastic seats also in the two-tone green colour.

The hired man looked at the boy and said, "Howdy ma'am, that's quite the get-up the boy's is wearing. You might wanna think about getting him something different to wear or he is gonna take an awful ribbing from other fellas his age." Mary looked at him and started to cry.

Jed Parker was annoyed with his hired man and said, "Let's git the hellos over and make Mary welcome before we give her advice on the Texas haberdashery. Let's get Mary and her boy home and settled before we dole out any more advice. OK?" The hired man took another look at the boy, rolled his eyes in disbelief and then when he got behind the wheel he had a little chuckle to himself, much to his employer's irritation.

Mary had stopped crying but was feeling decidedly overwhelmed although curious about this exciting new place. They turned north onto highway #10 as the wind was whipping through the old green Dodge since all of the windows were down. They were grateful as the heat was unbearable. Mary and Jimmy had never experienced heat like this in their entire lives. The radio was playing a country and western station and the song was Frankie's Man Johnnie, by Johnny Cash. The lyrics made Mary laugh; she'd never heard this kind of music. The giggle turned into a full-blown laugh until the hired man turned and looked at her and asked what she was laughing at.

She just turned a beet red from embarrassment and said, "Nothing." He was irritated with her laughing since he couldn't figure out what would be humorous. Even though he was being paid by Jed, he still felt annoyed with this uppity English girl. As the miles slipped by, every once in a while, a small western settlement dotted the highway. They passed the small town of Leon Springs and then they approached a larger town. Jed turned back to Mary and Jimmy, (the boy had fallen fast asleep) and said, "This town is Boerne. Our ranch is only a few miles from here." He turned back around and said nothing more for the rest of the journey.

They turned off highway #10 onto John's Road and as they travelled along the dirt road, the car kicked up billows of dust behind them. Then because of the vortex of wind, the dust began to come in the windows and covered them all in a fine blanket of dust. Young Mary put a hankie to her mouth and then grabbed her son and placed the cloth hankie over his mouth. She wondered to herself, *"Why have I come to this dirty, backward place?"*

The green Dodge Regent pulled up into the yard and there stood a large ranch style house with a huge covered veranda. On the veranda were seven or eight big rocking chairs and several small outside tables. There stood Jed's wife, wearing a big sweet smile with long grey hair tied in a bun. Even though she was a large woman she wore jeans, cowboy boots and the biggest blue earrings Mary had ever seen. Mary had never seen a woman wearing jeans and cowboy-boots. After all the hellos, introduction and hugs, Shirley put her arm into Mary's and said, "Com'on you sweet thing let's go inside."

They entered the ranch house and much to Mary's amazement it had a much lived in feel with a huge fieldstone fireplace adorned with the biggest pair of horns. It was a large open kitchen that housed a dining room with each room flowing into the next one. Mary had never seen a floor plan like this before and she liked it. Even though she was used to many small cold damp rooms shut off from each other, this had a friendly worn, lived-in feel to it.

Once inside and seated, Jed's wife, Shirley, offered her tea.

"Oh, thank you I could really do with a cup of tea." Shirley handed her a tall glass of ice with a bronze coloured drink and Mary took a sip and pulled a face.

"Oh, what is this?" she said without thinking.

"Tea," said Shirley.

"Oh, I thought you were offering me a cup of tea," said Mary.

"Would you like it served in a cup?" asked Shirley.

"No this is fine, thank you!" Mary thought the tea as they called it didn't resemble any tea she ever had before but decided to sip it and not say anything more.

"Mary, you and Jimmy must be tired."

"Yes, a little bit."

"Let's show them to the bunk house."

"I'll do that," volunteered Jed. Mary didn't know what a bunk house was and on the short walk to the old structure Jed explained that a bunk house was where the cowboys used to bunk while working on the ranch. Since they had no cowboys working the ranch anymore, and their only hired man had an apartment in town, the bunk house was only used for guests. Mary carried her suitcase, as did little Jimmy but mostly he dragged it and had to put it down occasionally and change hands. They approached an old smaller version of the main house that she'd come from, with a veranda and two rocking chairs positioned at the left end of the small veranda. They entered the building. It was painted with bright sunny colours and had lots of natural light. She loved it immediately. It had a small kitchen and one bedroom and a small living room. She loved the space and for the first time since she started this trip Mary felt the stress leaving her. "Where is the bathroom?" she asked. Jed pointed to an oval round tin tub hanging on the kitchen wall and he then opened the front door and motioned for her to follow him. They went behind the bunk house and there was a small wooden outhouse with a moon sawed neatly into the top of the door. Mary had no idea what it was so she turned the wooden latch holding the door shut and with that she was exposed to the worst smell. It immediately stung her eyes and made her cough. She quickly shut the door but didn't use the latch and it sprung open again exposing her to that wretched smell again. Jed laughed and said, "If the outhouse is too much for you Mary, you are welcome to use our inside restroom in the house." She just smiled and followed Jed back in the house.

He sat at the small kitchen table and said, "Tell me about my friend James Yeoman."

"My granddad is fine," she said.

He continued, "It's been such a long time. We were so young and James, I mean, your grandpa was so brave. I owe him my life you know."

"I know, he is truly a wonderful man, but it's hard for me to think of him as a young soldier," said Mary. "I've only known him as my granddad."

"I would love to see him again before I"...he stopped and started again..."it's just been so long. We have been sort of pen pals your grandfather and me."

"Actually you have been pen pals with my gran, James's wife; he has never been very comfortable writing so he tells her what to write." Jed stared at her for a moment and then laughed right from his belly, so much so that Mary started to laugh, while little Jimmy stared at them, wondering why on earth they were laughing. Jed left and walked slowly back to the main house feeling like he was well on his way to repaying an old outstanding debt. Jed was feeling quite satisfied with himself, and then he wondered how long this pretty young girl and her child would stay with them.

Some days passed. Mary and little Jimmy marvelled at all of the oddities that they saw. Every moment seemed to bring yet another revelation to them, some very foreign and some they liked very much. The people they met in town and visitors to the ranch were so helpful and welcoming, that Mary started to warm to the thought of spending many months perhaps even years in this place. Mary had managed to find loose tea at a local grocery store. That day she made herself a good old cuppa and took a minute to sit in the shade on the veranda of her little house when billows of dust approached on the horizon and slowly made its way up the long dirt driveway from John's Road to the ranch. Mary watched as a bright blue convertible Buick made its way into the yard. The car drove up on the grass right in front of the bunk house with

Mary sitting the veranda. She didn't know what to think, until she saw a very handsome man with dark curly hair and a smile that split his face from ear to ear!

"Howdy ma'am. My name is John Parker but mostly everyone calls me Jack. You must be that gal from England. I thought I'd take a few minutes to get my butt over here and introduce myself to you, but if I would have known how pretty you was, why I'da been here a lot quicker." As he smiled she saw a lot of his teeth.

Mary looked at him, and said, "Thank you."

Just then Shirley made her way from the main house to the bunk house in order to save Mary from her dandy of a nephew. "Jack Parker, what are you doing here?"

"Howdy Aunt Shirley you're looking beautiful as ever."

"Hush your mouth young man, your chin music is not playing with me. Now I thought you'd be sniffing around this young lady. You need to jump back in that Buick and head back down that dusty road."

"Ok Aunt Shirley but I'll be back; she is far too pretty to stay away from." Mary blushed and stared at her shoes until the convertible roared down the lane with billowing clouds of dust following the car.

"Mary that man is a playboy; do not listen to a word he says to you, do not be charmed by his chin music." "What is chin music?" asked a puzzled Mary. "His talk, is his chin music, that man has the gift of the gab, do you understand what I mean by that?" Mary smiled and answered quietly that she did but she had to admit to herself that she really liked the way he looked!

Two weeks passed and Mary received a good many letters as almost all the family was writing to her. They missed her but more importantly they knew she would be terribly homesick. Each letter was read and then she'd smell the letter for just a hint of a smell that was familiar and lovely. Then she'd read the letters again and again. She kept them all in a box and at night she'd lay in the bed and read them again. Sometimes she just looked at the return address and dreamed that she was there with them on the Friday night gathering at 173 Herbert Road. There, where everyone was treated to a sweet milky coffee and a visit, everyone referred to everyone else as 'Lovie' and James and Mary Yeoman would hold court. All of the daughters and their husbands would be there, as well as some of the nieces and nephews. She would play that recorded memory over and over in her mind until sleep would take her away. In the morning, she would wake with a fright and the realization that she was in rural Texas, thousands of miles away from everything and everybody she truly loved!

Chapter #12 *Relentless*

True to his word, the smiling Jack Parker found an excuse to head back over to Uncle Jed's ranch and that pretty little English girl. This time he drove uncharacteristically slowly so as to not cause a huge dust bowl. He didn't want to aggravate Aunt Shirley. He was fairly sure she didn't care much for him. He wandered around the yard and saw none of the family so made his way over to the bunk house and knocked on the wooden screened door. Mary came to the door and smiled as she saw that it was that young man with the blue convertible.

"Hello English miss," said Jack.

"Hello" said Mary quietly.

He said, "Can I come in?"

"What for?" asked Mary. "I thought I'd like to get to know you."

"I don't think your Aunt Shirley or Uncle Jed would like that." She pushed a little harder on the door to make sure the latch was on firmly, since she realized that she and little Jimmy were the only ones home at the ranch.

Jack instantly realized it too and he also understood that she was feeling vulnerable. "I'm sorry Mary. I really didn't know that no one was home. My aunt Shirley would skin me alive if she thought I'd do or say anything inappropriate to you. I'm going to leave so you don't have to feel…afraid. I'm really not that kind of man."

He went to step off the veranda and Mary opened the screen door and said, "It's okay you don't have to leave. You mustn't come indoors but we can have a little chat and sit on the veranda." Jack stopped and turned around.

This calculating man of the world knew exactly how to play his hand; he'd done it many times before. "No, Mary I won't allow you to feel even a little concerned about being here alone with me. I'll come back another time, when the family is around." She didn't disagree and he left with his usual smile and jumped into his dusty blue Buick and drove off. Mary was attracted to him and his dark curly hair and his huge grin. But she also noticed that he wore very loud, colourful clothing, bordering on outlandish.

Later that afternoon Jed and Shirley popped in to say hello to Mary and she told them that Jack had stopped by to see them.

"You see Jed I told you that nephew of yours was going to be a pest because Mary is here. He can't stay away from a pretty girl."

"Did he say or do anything to upset you?" asked Jed in a grandfatherly way.

"No he was very nice and very polite," answered Mary. "He said he was going to only come over here when you would both be here, so I didn't worry." Jed and Shirley just looked at each other as if to say, *that doesn't sound like Jack Parker.*

"He seems like a very nice bloke," announced Mary. Jed and Shirley were a little confused by the word 'bloke' but Shirley spoke first.

"Jack Parker is family Mary, but I need you to know that Jack makes his living from gambling, cards and poker! Jack Parker is a lady's man. Do you know what I'm saying Mary? He has been married and divorced twice and I've lost count of the number of girlfriends."

"Oh I see," said Mary "I didn't realize..."

Shirley cut her off, "Of course you wouldn't. Please Mary, be careful. Jed and I understand full well your circumstance and I'm sure I don't need to remind you that you are a married woman coming to Texas to get away from your criminal husband. To then get hooked up with the likes of Jack is akin to jumping out of the frying pan into the fire, if you get my meaning. I know he is a handsome man and you are a beautiful woman but believe me when I tell you Jack Parker Jr is trouble!"

She asked, "Why does he dress that way? I've seen him twice and he's always wearing very loud clothing?"

Jed was the first to respond. "Jack is a dandy. He loves to dress up in brightly coloured clothes but mostly it's because he is a golfer. If Jack isn't playing cards or chasing women, he'll be playing golf somewhere."

Mary was wondering how bad the man could be given the reaction of her hostess, but she made the decision to stay away from the handsome Jack Parker. Mary thanked Jed and Shirley.

A month into her new environment Jed wandered over to the bunk house after supper and asked if he could enter, "Yes, of course. It's your house," said Mary.

"Mary we are perfectly fine that you stay with us here at the ranch for as long as you require or want but for your own mental health and self-perseveration you'll have to be looking for work and some income of your own. What did you do in England?"

"I worked at Cundel's box factory and I was a barmaid at night." Somehow when she said it, she found herself ashamed of the work that she'd done to feed her family.

"Oh," said a surprised Jed Parker. He wasn't sure what to say, but he recovered after a time and said, "I'm sure there's plenty of work for a bright, lovely looking gal like you in Boerne."

"Uncle Jed," they had agreed on the first day that she'd call him Uncle Jed, "Can you give me a ride next time you go into the town?" "Yes of course I'm heading there tomorrow morning."

****

She felt decidedly out of place on Main Street with her best formal dress, red with gold Chinese dragons emblazoned every three inches and high heels, while every other female on Main Street was wearing jeans and cowboy boots or jeans and sneakers. Mary was determined to make her own way, and she had already seen that if she wanted a place of her own, or new clothes or two tickets back to England she'd have to work. She made the rounds to every restaurant, Mexican or otherwise and as she was making the rounds she heard that they were hiring at the restaurant at a golf course in Boerne. Mary was oblivious as to why a golf course would be hiring but if there was the possibility of a job she was going to apply. She understood it was outside of the town of Boerne and so took a cab with the last of her money. As she entered the dining room part of the golf club she was met by the chief cook, who was a large bellied, pompous Greek man that looked her up and down and smiled at her in a way that made her feel uncomfortable.

She smiled sweetly at him and said "I understand you are hiring. I'm looking for work any kind of work." She stopped and took a breath and thought, *"I'll take anything, any job."*

The big Greek man said, "Hired. You'll work in the kitchen with me," and then he winked at her.

"I think I'd prefer to be a waitress," responded Mary, afraid of what the wink meant. He said, "Kitchen work or no work, your choice, girly."

Mary said, "Thank you. When do I start?"

"Tomorrow at 6 am, don't be late." She melted out of the dining room into the parking lot and noticed a Blue Buick convertible. She stood staring at the car wondering how on earth she was going to get to the town, never mind back out to the ranch. She waited, and waited and was eventually rewarded by two golf carts racing up the 18th fairway with a person dressed entirely in red; red trousers, white golf shoes with a red saddle, red golf shirt and he even wore a red golf glove. She put her hand to her mouth to stop herself from laughing out loud at the comical sight. Jack Parker spotted her immediately and jumped off the moving golf cart and ran over to her as she was sitting under a live oak tree on her coat. He looked at her under the tree in her form fitted red dress with the dragons and her long brunette hair rolled and falling into her lap. She was even more attractive than he remembered.

"Mary, what are you doing here? Are you waiting for me?"

"Well, sort of. I was hoping you could give me a ride back to the ranch. I've been looking for work and the gentleman inside has hired me as his cook's helper, starting tomorrow at 6 am. I used the last of my American dollars to take a cab out here."

"Well you gorgeous child, he ain't no gentlemen. It would be my honour and privilege to give a lady of such beauty a ride in my big blue chariot." Mary thought to herself *there is that chin music again!* She laughed at him and felt comfortable enough to tell him he looked very red and he took it as a compliment. Mary thought perhaps it was. She was grateful for a ride back to the ranch and her Jimmy and the bunk house.

"Mary why are you going to be that Greek creep's gopher?"

"That is the only job he had, I need work, I have to earn my way. Uncle Jed was very clear on that point."

"Wait here in the car," Jack jumped out and raced back to the clubhouse. He came back in about twenty minutes and said, "You start tomorrow at 10 am as a waitress and I'll be your ride until we can make other arrangements." Mary looked over and saw the big Greek man scowling at them out of the kitchen window.

"I hope you haven't made that bloke wild at me," said Mary. Jack looked at her and paused and said, "Mary the owner of the golf club is a very good friend of mine; he owes me a lot of favours. I explained the situation to my friend and our Greek friend knows that if he causes you one minute of grief or fear, he'll be the one looking for work!" With that Jack winked at her and roared off to deposit Mary at the Parker's ranch. As they rode along in the blue convertible with the wind blowing her hair every which way, she felt like a movie star, sitting next to a very handsome and now very protective friend...Jack Parker Jr.

Mary retold the entire story to Shirley and Jed and they just looked at each other with that knowing look that says that Jack Parker had finally wormed his way into this girl's heart and life. True to his word, Jack Parker picked her up every morning and after her shift was over he'd run her the five miles back to the ranch.

"Mary, have you thought about taking a place in town or buying a car?"

"I can't drive."

"I'll teach you," announced Jack. After the first driving lesson in the Buick they sat on the small veranda with a glass of ice tea. Mary was starting to acclimatize to Texas' favourite drink.

"Mary, you must know that I'm falling for you."
"You can't Jack, I'm married", said Mary with as much enthusiasm as she could muster. She knew she had feelings for the handsome philanderer, but she was afraid.

"Are you planning to go back to England and back into that situation that you have escaped from?"

"I don't know Jack. I like Texas but I miss my family terribly and some nights I ache so much to see them that my chest actually hurts." He knew her resistance was breaking down. He could feel it. So he thought a few more patient driving lessons, and rides back and forth to work and she'll cave.

He smiled at her and said, "You did well at your first driving lesson. I'll pick you up tomorrow morning and drive you to work. We can do another lesson after work."

She smiled at him, and said, "Thank you." She paused and he almost thought she was going to kiss him but she said, "You'd better get home." Jack knew he was close.

Chapter #13 Acclimate

Mary had eight driving lessons and much to her surprise and despite her nervous disposition seemed to get the hang of it after just a few lessons. She enjoyed her time with Jack; he and his incessant chin music was always so much fun. Driving was easy on the quiet Texas back roads but getting into traffic of any kind even when it was the light traffic in the town of Boerne became much more challenging. She had no choice, so she kept at it and became a mildly competent driver. It was another typical morning, waiting for Jack to arrive in his blue Buick to drive her the five miles to the golf course to wait on the people that golfed and had lunch, and the business people that took clients and friends to lunch at the club. Mary stood waiting by the veranda where Jack usually picked her up. Jimmy took the school bus every morning and Shirley loved to look after him after school. She had become his de-facto Texas grandma.

Mary was looking forward to seeing Jack's handsome face and big smile.

Shirley came running out of the big house, "Jack has been shot."

Mary stood there almost frozen like she did when her father had died. She couldn't process the information.

"Mary, Jack has been shot! I'll drive you to work."
"Where is he?" shouted back Mary, she had gained some of her senses back, but was still shaking uncontrollably.

"He's at the Boerne Hospital. I knew this was going to happen one day; he can't keep playing with fire and not expect to get burnt. I can't help but love that boy, but I'd truly like to strangle him some days, and this is one of them." They raced to the hospital and arrived at Jack's room. They found two sheriff's deputies coming out of his room and Shirley said, "What happened. I'm his aunt."

"Your family is in with him. They'll fill y'all in," he said casually. Shirley and Mary walked into the room to find several people already there including Jack's aging mother and father, and a very garish looking gal with far too much makeup, a low-cut blouse and huge breasts that seemed to be straining to get out of her blouse.

"Howdy, I'm Jack's girlfriend Ionia", she announced as she stood to greet Mary and Shirley. Mary thought that at least one of her boobs was going to pop out of their resting place and she wanted to giggle but resisted.

Shirley shook her hand but said nothing as she turned toward Jack and said, "What happened?"

He looked sore but smiled and said, "Someone took a dislike to my handsome good looks."

"Come on young man what happened?"

"Someone drove up as I was leaving the hotel last night and shot at me. I lifted my hands to protect myself and the gun went off and the bullet hit me in the shoulder."

"Did you see who shot you?" Shirley pressed.

"I didn't" he said but she knew better.

"You are going to be the death of your mother and father from simply worry." Jack tried to move the conversation to something less focused on him and his unfortunate circumstance. Mary just stood away from the bed and the people sitting around the bed. Meanwhile Jack couldn't take his eyes off her and Ionia knew it.

"Who is she?" asked Ionia as she pointed at Mary. Her breasts jiggled and bounced. Jack's father Jack Parker Sr. just stared at her hoping that just once they'd bounce out of her blouse.

"I live at Shirley and Jed's ranch and Jack has been helping me to learn to drive" she said in a defensive manner.

"I'm damn sure he has been hepin you. You stay away from my Jack. We are getting married.

Shirley ushered Mary out of the room and said, "Come on Mary I'll drive you to work. You'll be late but at least you'll get to work."

"Thanks." She was grateful to make her exit and on her way out said, "I wish you better Jack." But Mary never looked at Jack for fear of Ionia.

******

"You see Mary, Jack is a born Casanova, he just can't help himself!" Mary smiled and said, "Yes I know," as she tried to hide the trembling from the verbal confrontation she received from the gal with the big boobs.

Shirley dropped off Mary and made her way back to Jack's hospital room and she found him alone. "Did you tell the police who it was Jack?"

"No I don't know who it was."

"Yes you do. It was the Levinson boys. If you continue playing cards with them, it is going to be the death of you young man."

Jack wasn't feeling very young any more. The bad marriages and failed relationships were one thing but making a living from poker was wearing, even on him, and now being shot by the Levinson boys. Aunt Shirley was right, as usual, those bastards were out to kill him. They had taken this whole thing to another level. Fear was an unusual emotion for Jack Parker. The Levinson brothers knew he was cheating at cards; no one could be that lucky. The problem was they couldn't catch him at it!

Shirley continued to drive Mary to and from her job. Mary had scheduled her driving test and with any luck she would be able to pass the exam and then drive from the ranch through the rocky hills dotted with live oak trees that hung heavy with moss. She thought the moss looked like old men's beards. She was starting to love the hill country of south Texas. It looked so mysterious to the gal from East London. Her former life was starting to be a fading memory of old brick factory buildings. Familiar faces were all melding into one distant memory as the daily needs and challenges of Texas life seemed to absorb her thoughts. She found herself thinking less and less about her life back home and the visceral fear that sent her off to America was only frightening to her when she allowed herself to drift backward in time. Her husband, the big Englishman didn't frighten her any more. She felt safe with the almost certainty that he'd never travel to America, never mind Texas, to find her.

Jimmy, who was growing into a pre-teen, seemed to acclimatize to life in Texas. His cockney east end accent got him attention at school, which he enjoyed especially from the girls. While not a great student he passed most subjects, just! Jack had left after the shooting, some said to Dallas, some Houston, it didn't matter. Mary missed him and she wondered if he left with Ionia or by himself. Mary had passed the driving test and had purchased a refurbished 1958 Dodge Royal. It, too, was green inside and out. It had a push button automatic transmission and the biggest fins at the rear of the car. Mary thought it looked a little like a spaceship with its clear plastic steering wheel and its AM-stereo radio. Mary couldn't be more proud to be driving into town in her own car, as long as she was able to keep the payments up, even if it was a green Dodge!

Jimmy required far fewer stories these days; although from time to time he still liked to request a family story with his hot sweet cup of tea. His mother was always ready to indulge him. He heard the same stories over and over but never tired of them. Life had become mundanely steady at the ranch. Jed was moving slower than he did those many months ago when she arrived. Shirley was still as feisty as ever and Mary had grown to love her even though from time to time she was a little too direct for comfort.

The letters from family still arrived but with far less frequency than when she had first come to the ranch, but she was always grateful for them. Shirley handed her the mail or the post as Mary called it. It was a warm cloudless morning; the blue sky was so bright that as she looked up skyward to take in the piercing blueness it hurt her eyes. She could never remember one day in England when she saw the sky that blue and cloudless. Two letters on that thin blue airmail paper with familiar writing meant that she was going to enjoy the news from home. *I'll save them for later tonight to enjoy with a nice cup of tea.* The other piece of mail was from the British Red Cross. She looked at it and was curious but didn't understand why the Red Cross would send her a letter. *Perhaps they were looking for a donation.* As she read the letter she began to shake, then the shaking became more like a vibration and she dropped the letter in shock.

Shirley was standing next to her and grabbed her arm, "What on earth is wrong my child?" said Shirley her eyes as big as they could possibly get.

"He has found me, he has found me," she just kept repeating. Mary put her hands to her eyes and cried. Shirley picked up the letter and read it. The Red Cross had a program that helped estranged relatives find missing and lost loved ones. Even though she had used her maiden name in Texas, the Red Cross had found her and they were encouraging her to please get in touch with her loving relative. They supplied his name and address. It was her old address. Mary was still sobbing and still shaking.

"Come on now missy, he ain't found you, he is just fishing. All you gotta do is not respond. He'll go back into the past where he belongs." Mary wasn't so sure. They went into the big house and Shirley insisted that Mary have a good strong cup of coffee. Mary shuddered as she drank it.

Later that night with fear now her ever present companion she sat on the veranda pushing slowly back on the rocking chair. She took a sip of her hot, sweet tea and leaned her head back, her legs were aching. She wondered how many miles she walked in a day back and forth from the kitchen to tables all day long. She thought of all the regulars and how they teased her about her accent and called her honey child and baby doll. She liked most of them and looked forward to seeing them. She opened the first letter, given the hand writing she knew it was from Lily the English aunt with the club foot. She read the words, *"Lovie, I'm so sad to let you know that your dear granddad has died. He left us quietly in his sleep and didn't suffer at all."* There was more news about the funeral and how the family was coping with his death but it was lost on Mary. Her beloved, patriarchal grandfather was gone and she was robbed of spending these last years with him because of her husband. She hated him so severely and completely at that moment that she stopped the rocking chair and stood up involuntarily. She squeezed the letter so tightly that it hurt her fingers. Then she just sat and wept loudly. The next day she went over to the big house and found Jed as she usually did sitting on the veranda. He was on his third cup of black Folgers coffee.

"Uncle Jed."
"Yes," responded Jed.
"My granddad has passed away."
"I know honey child."
"How did you know?"
"I heard your grief last night." His bottom lip started to quiver, and big tears filled his old eyes. He tried to say more but was unable so he just stared off into the calico coloured hills of the ranch. Mary called into work to tell them that she was unable to make it that day. She told them she wasn't feeling well. She didn't tell them her heart was breaking.

Days, then weeks passed and Mary told herself she needed to try to save money for a ticket home to see her family before much more time went by. Before, God forbid, any more of her loves passed away. But she knew she couldn't go back to her life in England because of the fear waiting for her there. That fear was now looking for her even in this far off place of Texas. Fear was starting to control her daily life; she was imagining him jumping out at her from around every corner and in every dark place. Her imagination was getting the better of her even at work. A customer would ask her a mundane question like, "Do you have any plans for the weekend?" Instead of answering normally she asked them why they were asking her about her personal life which didn't exactly ingratiate her with her regulars that she had become so fond of.

It was a very warm evening and as Mary usually did after Jimmy went to bed she meandered out onto the veranda with a cup of tea, with milk and loaded with sugar.
Mary loved the veranda on these warm and sultry nights, not a breath of air was moving. She could feel the

sweat rolling down from her neck and shoulders on to her blouse. She wondered if the veranda hadn't become her most favourite place in the world. She could hear the radio playing a country and western tune. She knew that Jed would be in the rocking chair over at the big house with a big mug of Folgers. If Shirley wasn't watching he would sneak a little bourbon into the Folgers. Shirley didn't take to his drinking alcohol lightly; she had made her feelings known to Jed for fifty-eight years. Jed was respectful of her opinions but he loved the way a pour of bourbon relaxed him in the evening and somehow it helped the stiffness and pain of being in his eighties. He was sure the good Lord and even Shirley would forgive him for this small indulgence. Weeks had passed since she and Jed had received the news that James Yeoman had passed away, but Mary hadn't really been able to speak about her granddad. She felt that it was time to remember him with his old friend. She wanted to go over and tell him stories about James Yeoman, for him, but really for herself! Mary wandered over to the big house and managed her way up the five stairs and walked toward Jed on his favourite rocking chair. Jed was leaning his head back and smiling. She had become so fond of her granddad's friend.

 She sat comfortably in the chair and across from him and said, "Uncle Jed I've been thinking of your friend James Yeoman tonight and what a wonderful, granddad, husband and father he was. I remember the time when"...she stopped.

 "Uncle Jed, Uncle Jed," she stood, and pleaded to the warm South Texas air...Please no! Shirley opened the screen door and said, "What's all the commotion out here?" Shirley approached Jed from the back not realizing he was gone.

 She came around, saw Mary's tears and disbelief. She grabbed his arm and went to her knees wailing, "No, please God, no!" The pleading lasted for minutes until Mary bravely walked over and dropped to the floor of the veranda and put her arms around Shirley. They rocked in unison back and forth for a time, until Shirley broke free and stood up. "Mary this moment I have feared every day for the past fifty-eight years. I was nothing until this beautiful, kind man loved me and much to my delight made me his family. I've loved him more than words can say." She wept again. She and Mary hugged again. Nothing more needed to be said!

The days and hours all blurred into each other and Mary forgot about her daily fear. She tried to be with and watch over Shirley as much as her time and Shirley would allow. The funeral was planned and Shirley knew many people would want to come to the wake. She requested just close family and friends be at the internment. Jed was going to be buried beside his father and mother on the ranch; she knew he'd be pleased with that arrangement. Hundreds of people would show up for the wake. They put up a big white tent that the church had loaned them. "The church uses it for outside prayer meetings and come to Jesus meetings", said the Reverend Duet to Mary when she accompanied Shirley to make the arrangements. Mary didn't know what 'come to Jesus meetings' were so she just smiled at the silver haired minister.

Chapter #14 *Running scared*

It was a warm windy day in the south Texas hill country, more hot than warm. You could smell the pollen from the cedar trees being carried on the warm wind. As Shirley knew they would, hundreds of people showed up to the wake at the ranch, most giving the usual regrets at Jed's passing and remembering him as the good man, neighbour, or friend. Shirley took time for them all. As the afternoon came to a close the crowds started to dissolve, until finally only family, a few very close friends and the minister were left. The actual burial was to be at sunset as per Jed's request, his favourite time of the day. Just as they were making their way to the burial site off in the distance they saw billows of dust and a red car making its way up the long approach.

Shirley said, "It's Jack, I knew he'd come, I couldn't be more pleased." Sure enough as the the bright red 1964 Ford Galaxy 500 convertible made its way into the yard, Mary could see the handsome dark curls hanging in his eyes and the contagious smile that seemed to completely split his face. She hadn't realized how much she had missed him. Shirley ran up to the car, "Jack, thank you for coming, you've made me very happy and I know your Uncle Jed would be pleased to know you came too!" Jack hugged his aunt Shirley for a long time and then his mother and father. He joined the group walking to the burial site.

He looked over to Mary. She smiled at him, and he thought *how beautiful she looked.* "Hello my little English miss," he said quietly as they walked. "You didn't bring your girlfriend."

"What girlfriend?"

"Ionia." "I never saw her again after that day in the hospital." Mary cocked her head to the side and smiled at him in mocking disbelief. "It's true, she was...not the girl for me...you are Mary." *Chin music,* thought Mary. After the funeral they all gathered on the veranda at the big house and Jack sat next to her on the double rocker. "How's Jimmy doing at school?" he asked her.

"He's doing well. I'm sure he's over at the bunk house watching TV. Why not go over and have a chat with him before you leave."

"I will, but my leaving will be up to you."

"Jack I'm not going to be one of your many women that you use and then cast then aside."

"I would never cast you aside Mary, I've never met anyone like you."

She laughed at him. "How many ladies have to you told that line to?"

"Quite a few but I've never meant it before now." She discounted his comment by telling him, "Make sure you go over and say goodbye to Jimmy before you go."

Mary had taken a few days off from her work at the dining room to help Shirley with the funeral arrangements. The day after dispatching Jed she got up late but got Jimmy to the bus on time and in her nightdress and housecoat she made her way over to the big house to have a coffee with Shirley and to check up on her. She knew the next few days would be tough. Shirley tried to busy herself as though being busy would negate the horrendous loss.

"Mary, here is your mail." Mary took the envelope and noticed it was from England but didn't recognise the writing. She opened the letter and read the first paragraph. The words stuck in her mind as though they were jagged and rough. She read words like: *Even though I can't come to America right now, I'd like you to get in touch with me. If I don't hear from you, I'm going to send someone over there to find you.*

She quickly folded the letter and shoved it into her housecoat pocket; she didn't want Shirley to have to worry about this on top of losing her Jed. She made her excuses, something about ironing, and made her way to the bunk house. Mary was in a spin. Fear had found her now and nothing or no one was going to save her. She had to run and run fast.

Mary went from room to room but did nothing; she was so overcome by fear that she couldn't focus. When a knock at the door came, she jumped from the shock of it. *It's him* she thought, *his people are here!* She stood in the middle of the small main room in the bunk house and trembled and started to cry.

"Mary, it's Jack."

She stopped, and said, "Jack Parker is that you?"

"Can I come in Mary?"

"Yes Jack please, come in." Jack still smiling entered the bunk house to find his little English Miss still in her house coat and slippers, her hair sticking up and sticking out, no make-up and crying profusely.

"Mary what on earth is the matter?" She told him the whole story. It didn't take long and Jack said, "You and Jimmy are coming with me; we need to get out of here and fast!"

Mary said, "Are you sure? It might be dangerous if he ever finds us"...she paused..."together."

Jack said, "I'll take that chance. Let's grab some clothes and things for Jimmy. You'll know what you want to take as we likely won't be back this way for a long time."

"Where will we go?" Mary looked pathetic as Jack took her in his arms and tried to reassure her he'd look after her no matter what.

Jack thought, *of all the times I've dreamt of holding her I didn't dream she'd look like this*, he smiled to himself. "OK,

Mary, you go and pick up Jimmy from school. I have to make some arrangements myself. You'll have to let Aunt Shirley know. She's not going to be too pleased that you're going to be with me, Mary, you know that, right?" Mary looked at him in her dazed yet manic state and said, "I'll speak with her."

"Mary I'll be back tonight at supper time. We'll take your car. Mine is a little too conspicuous and it will be easy to sell. I know just the guy who will give me cash for it today. We are going to need cash."

Adrenalin caused Jack to jump off the veranda, he didn't use the stairs at all, and then into the red Ford Galaxy. He regretted having to give it up. It was a head turner to be sure but he wanted Mary more than he wanted to turn heads. He wondered to himself if she was the one that would make him settle down. He'd had that thought with many women in his life. He hoped this time was different. He hoped he wasn't just kidding himself and her. It really didn't matter. He wasn't letting this opportunity to be with this woman slip out of his grip regardless of the ultimate outcome.

After a quick hair wash in the kitchen sink, a bit of makeup and hair spray, Mary was finally able to focus and place into suitcases what she needed to for both her and Jimmy. She wondered how he'd react, but the one thing she knew was that her son had the same irrational fear of the big man. He'd had many nightmares, the kind that woke Mary with a fright and she had to wake him just to settle him down. She was sure once Jimmy knew there was a possibility that the big man knew where they lived; he'd want to leave the ranch too.

Shirley watched Jack drive off creating billows of dust all the way down the approach to Johns Road on the way out to Highway #10. She wondered why he left so quickly and eventually made her way slowly over to the bunk house. She knocked and walked in, which was her usual habit.

Mary was just exiting the bedroom, she had a towel wrapped around her head and was still wearing her terry towel housecoat. "Oh Shirley I was going to come and see you. I have something to tell you, I'm leaving!"

Shirley was taken aback and got even more feisty than usual. "What... Mary I don't understand why you are talking about leaving." Mary took the letter out of her housecoat and handed it to Shirley. She read it and just looked up at Mary not knowing what to say.

"You see I told you he knows where I am and he'll not rest until he finds me. I'm really afraid *he'll do me in.*"

"You mean kill you Mary?"

"Yes that's exactly what I mean."

"Can he be that bad?" Shirley asked in resignation. Mary looked lovingly at Shirley; her eyes were tired, sad and old. She was still reeling from the biggest loss of her life and now Mary was dropping this on her.

"Where will you go?"

"I'm going with Jack; I know you won't be pleased with that decision."

"No Mary you are wrong, I've always loved my nephew Jack Parker, even though he has driven me completely crazy over the years. If Jack stays with you, you couldn't be in better hands. Jack knows every way to make you impossible to find, but your challenge is going to be keeping his roving eye in check."

Mary smiled and said, "Yes I believe you are right." Mary and Shirley hugged and both cried.

Shirley took a long look at Mary and said, "I've come to love you child." Mary cried and hugged the old woman again.

Chapter #15 *A safe place*

"Jack, tell me again where are we going?"

"Covington, Louisiana. It's where I've been living these past few months, since the shooting. It's only an hour's drive to Baton Rouge and I've found a few good tables in the city."

"What do you mean tables?" "Mary, you must know I'm a professional gambler; I make my living with a deck of cards and poker is my game. I used to throw dice for a living but making money from poker is way more fun and much more lucrative."

"Isn't it a little dangerous?"

Jack smiled his cheeky smile and said, "Maybe a little." Mary turned her head and just looked out of the car window as they drove through the night in her 58 Dodge Royale. Jimmy had fallen asleep in the back seat in amongst the pans, tea towels and house wares thrown into the back seat. The huge trunk was stuffed to capacity with suitcases and personal items. Mary wondered what was going to become of them running away yet again with this man.

Then she thought of what her dear friend Shirley said, *"Jack knows every way to make you impossible to find, your challenge is going to keep his roving eye in check."* She smiled to herself and slipped into a deep sleep. They slipped through Houston and onto Baton Rouge and finally to the small sleepy town of Covington. Jack pulled up to a three-storey stick built apartment block, clad in aluminum siding with some faux brick accent. The north side of the building had a hint of green moss, a sure sign that this building wasn't well cared for. The dead grass and lack of any landscaping confirmed that fact.

Jack turned off the engine of the old green Dodge and looked over at Mary, sleeping soundly and then back at the now adolescent boy in the back seat and thought, "*Do I want this responsibility?*" He looked back at her and said out loud, "Yup I do!"

He opened the car door and Mary woke with a fright, "Where are we?"

"Home," said Jack, "Come upstairs and see the apartment. It's definitely not as nice as your bunk house but it will do until I can find us something better." Mary woke Jimmy and they all climbed the three flights of stairs to apartment 302. Jack opened the door and the smell rushed out, a stale, male smell. All of the curtains were closed. It was not only smelly but dark, which hid the fact that the sink was full to overflowing with dishes and Jack's clothes covered every available chair, couch, and lamp. Jack was grateful that none of his lady friends had left any telltale garments lying around. Mary looked at him with that "what-on-earth-look" and he just tilted his head to one side and said, "I'm not much of housekeeper Mary."

Mary put her hand on her hips and said, "I can see that."

Jack put on the coffee pot and said, "Mary I'm going to get a few groceries for you and the boy. Then this afternoon I have to leave."

"What, where are you going?" replied Mary in a panic.

"Baton Rouge, I have to work. I have to get in on a table."

Mary didn't really understand but was so grateful that Jack had extricated her from a fear that she was unable to deal with, that she just said "Okay, when will you be back?"

"Sometime tomorrow. I'll have to take your car, okay?"

Before she realized what she was doing she said, "Okay."

Mary started by opening every curtain and window that would open. Then she cleaned, washed, polished and shined everything in the small one-bedroom apartment. She washed every towel, ironed and hung shirts. All that day she cleaned and made everything look and most importantly smell clean and fresh. Jimmy never moved off the couch or away from the TV. She asked him twice for help but he made a teenage excuse both times. Mary thought to herself, *he is becoming a man, they are all lazy!*

As the evening descended on Mary and Jimmy, she wondered when Jack would get back. It was then it struck her - *what about sleeping arrangements?*

She had washed all the blankets and sheets on Jack's bed. There was only one bedroom. She looked at the couch and was relieved to find it was a hide-a-bed. She made up a bed for Jimmy and took the cushions off the couch and made a bed for herself on the floor beside Jimmy.

"Mum."

"Yes my boy."

"Can you tell me a story?"

"It's been a long time since you asked me for a story."

"I know, I'm feeling a bit sad being in this place. It's not very nice Mum."

"I know son but it's better than living in fear that he'll find us, right?"

"Yes."

She wanted to change the subject. "Have I told you about Aunt Maud's Uncle Frank and what he did during the war?"

"No."

"He was in tanks in Germany."

"He fought with Monty."

"Mum, who is, Monty?"

"General Bernard Montgomery the famous tank general that chased Hitler's troops as they retreated from Normandy in France back all the way to Germany."

"Was Uncle Frank married to Aunt Maud then?"

"Yes he was. Uncle Frank was a gunner in the 3rd Armoured Division. "

Frank was a tall, frightfully thin man, who looked like he needed a few good meals. He had a thin mustache on his upper lip; which he had seen being worn by a handsome movie star on the silver screen. When his wife Maud told him she thought the movie star was handsome, Frank had worn one ever since. He was a nervous man and not sure of himself. This nervous disposition caused his trigger finger to be twitchy, not a good quality for a gunner. They were pushing the Germans and their tanks back across France and Holland as they retreated to Germany.

*****

The ground shook as a roaring, grinding noise developed. The shrubs rustled and then bent to the ground as the big Sherman tanks pushed their way through the French countryside. They were looking for a particular German Panzer tank that was trying desperately to avoid the Allied counter offensive which now operated with a two to one advantage. The tank commander had given Frank's group the mission to find and destroy a rogue Panzer tank that had caused despair and grief near the French town of Caen. Instead of moving back with the rest of the Panzer unit, this particular tank was operating independently of the Panzer retreat. The information that was circulating throughout the British units was that these were hardened tank soldiers that knew that Germany was about to fall. They were not planning to be taken alive, which was borne out of the terrible atrocities they were committing with the French citizenry. The commander had sent two Sherman tanks to seek and destroy this marauding tank. On the second day, the British unit comprising of the two Sherman tanks spotted a German renegade tank hiding in a small village and Frank's tank was moving in on the target. Meanwhile, the second British tank was coming into the village from the opposite direction. The Panzer tank was hiding behind a tall brick wall that was a remnant of the sturdy brick factory that had taken a direct hit. One wall was all that was left of the tire factory. Frank's shaky hand was on the trigger and his eyes were glued to the sight. He was breathing heavily. Then he saw the muzzle of the big German gun sticking out in front of the brick wall, and he yelled, "Right!" and fired. The rest of the crew inside Frank's tank were instantly focused and the commander saw the Panzer muzzle at the same time as Frank and was relieved that he hit the trigger. He automatically yelled, "Reload, reload!" Frank's loader, a small man from Liverpool, swore as the shell ejected and his task was to load the next deadly missile into the breach. The initial shell hit the brick wall and it slowed the armour piercing tank killer down just enough that when it burst through the brick wall it hit the track of the tank, which simply disintegrated the track, making the huge German tank immoveable. In the meantime, the remaining brick wall fell onto the tank. The turret of the German machine was trying to turn toward Frank's tank but couldn't because of the massive amount of brick that was lodged on top of the tank.

  The tank commander screamed, "Fire at will! They are trying to take up aim directly at us!"

  Frank forgot to change his aim and in his panic he simply pressed the trigger. The second shot hit in exactly the same place but without the brick wall to slow it down, it hit the lower portion of the tank and the turret stopped trying to turn towards them. After a moment the lid of the tank opened and a German solider popped up waving a rifle with a dirty ragged white shirt attached to the muzzle end of the rifle.

The tank commander said, "Frank keep your hand on that trigger. It might be a trick." One by one the five occupants of the German tank got out and stood in a line with their hands in the air. The one with the shirt on the rifle threw the gun with the shirt still attached to the ground and put his hands above his head and began to gingerly climb down to join his comrades. Just at that point the second tank arrived and out came the crew.

Frank was the last person to leave his tank. They made sure there weren't any more Panzer tanks lurking about. Frank was walking toward the Germans standing in a line still with their hands above their heads. As he got closer to them he realized that these weren't men but boys in German uniforms. Two of them weren't any older than thirteen.

He was dumbstruck. "These are just lads," said Frank's tank commander. "How could they have been mistaken for war worn soldiers?" They checked them over for weapons of hand guns and knives, and discovered several of each. The leader of the group who looked to be sixteen or seventeen chaffed at having a very large dagger found in his boot. He grabbed at the solider that took it off him, and the commander of the other tank rifled butted him in the face. It obviously broke not only the skin but his cheekbone too. Frank blanched at the unnecessary use of blunt force. The young German spat into the face of the other British tank commander, and was hit again, this time harder. Frank wasn't able to stand it and without thinking said, "Oye, that's enough he's only a boy!"

"Only a boy," said the now incensed tank commander. He moved quickly and aggressively toward Frank and poked Frank in the chest very hard as he told him that any more of his mouth and he would be reported for insubordination as well as get a bloody good hiding for good measure. Frank moved backward. He could see that this tank commander was mean and war hardened. Frank was afraid of him. Just then the German boy bleeding from two vicious cracks from the Royal Enfield 303 rifle butt took off on the run. The tank commander slowly lifted his 303 and shot him squarely in the back of the head. His cap flew into the air and he fell lifeless onto the ground.

Frank put his hands to his face and exclaimed, "Oh, my dear God."

His tank superior grabbed the shooter and shouted at him, "What are you doing, you stupid bastard? You're going to have us all in trouble."

The shooter just smiled and said, "I 'ad no choice. The prisoner was trying to escape." Then he looked at Frank and winked. Frank stood there hanging between revulsion and white madness. Then he was suddenly overcome with the pointlessness and ignobility of this war that he had believed in and signed up for. They radioed for the prisoners to be picked up and they stood guard until the lorry and the MP's showed up. But the young Germans were not going anywhere or trying anything after what they had witnessed.

Jimmy had trouble sleeping after hearing this unusual story. It kept rolling over and over in his mind. He hoped he never had to go to war.

Chapter #16 Time for a change

Jack got back to the apartment at 4 am, half expecting but more hoping that Mary would be in his bed. She wasn't. As he entered the one-bedroom apartment he saw Jimmy on the hide-a-bed and then he realised that Mary was on the floor beside the hide-a-bed. He leaned over, woke her up and led her to the bedroom. She was in a state of sleep but as they got to the bedroom door she froze, realising what was happening.

Jack, much to his own surprise said, "It's alright my little English miss, I'll sleep on the hide-a-bed with Jimmy. You have the bed." She didn't argue, quickly got under the covers and immediately went sound asleep. He lay on the hide-a-bed after pushing Jimmy over to one side and smiled, looking up at the ceiling. It had been a good night; they would have no money worries for a while. Then he noticed the place smelled…clean!

The days that followed saw Jimmy enrolled in school and Mary got a job at the bakery, serving coffee, corn beef hash, eggs and grits and such to the locals on Main Street in Covington. They loved her English accent, and made fun of her in a fun and neighbourly way. Jack realised that he needed to look for a two bedroom apartment sooner than later. Jimmy was starting to lose his English accent and all the attention that went with it. Sometimes he'd tried to get it back but try as he might he was sounding more and more every day like an American. He was a nondescript young man; he was never a stand out at anything. He played a little basketball and baseball and was only average at both. His grades were the same beige and bland, forty-eight to fifty-two percent on every test and year end marks. Most people couldn't recall him or remember his name. He was a dreamy kid and when he was alone he'd pretend that his real father would show up like in the Charles Dickens novel and claim his son. He knew better. All Mary would tell him was that his father didn't know about his existence and would likely be embarrassed by him; his father thought he was far too good for the likes of them. Try as he might she would not tell stories about his own father, she used uncharacteristically blunt and hurtful words when she spoke of Jimmy's real father.

Jack Parker was spending several nights a week in Baton Rouge at the tables and most nights he scored, sometimes not much but enough to keep the wolf from the door. On the odd occasion he came home as a loser but he was skilled enough to know not to chase a losing night. If he got on a small losing slide he played very carefully or simply excused himself. Most of the participants were not professionals; every night there were different people that wanted to try their luck, some drunk on liquor, others drunk on ego or sometimes just plain stupidity. Jack and the other professionals could almost always take full advantage of every weakness in players that showed up with money to gamble with.

Jack was impressed with the way Mary was able to take care of everything, the apartment and in their lives. She wasn't like the other women he'd married or shared his life with. Those gals were ready to party any time, and anywhere. He'd lived in the same place as this English gal; she was such a homemaker, that he wondered what drew him to her. They found and moved into a two-bedroom apartment in the same complex but they did not share a bed.

Jack was starting to think perhaps he should be looking for a girlfriend. "Mary, we are living together as husband and wife, yet not, if you get my meaning."

"Yes Jack, I understand your meaning completely. When the time is right I will share your bed. If you'd like me and Jimmy to move out I will."

"No, Mary I don't want that at all. That is the last thing I want. I'm off to the golf course, I have a game."

"Jack, do you play golf for money too?"

"Mary, everything I do is for money or some kind of pay-off." She understood the hidden meaning of that statement. Since Jimmy was at school, he was able to speak openly to her. "Mary, when will the time be right."

"When I'm sure it's for love Jack and not just lust."

Jack moved toward her and said, "I'm sure I love you Mary."

Mary looked up at him and said, "It's me that needs to be sure." Jack left for the golf course.

Weeks passed. One day, Mary awoke and found Jack's bedroom door closed and thought nothing of it. She got Jimmy going that morning which continued to be a chore; he still hated getting out of his bed even though he was now a teenager and getting close to six feet tall. She headed off to her job at the bakery café. Jimmy watched the TV while he ate his breakfast, which his mother had warned him not to. Jack's bedroom door opened and he stepped out. Jimmy looked up to catch him falling against the door jamb. Jimmy was shocked and jumped up and ran toward Jack.

He held him up and got him to the couch. "Jack what happened?"

Jack tried to smile at the boy but the pain made it turn to a grimace. He had so many cuts and scrapes on his face and he had congealed blood in his hair and down his neck. But most of the pain was his side that he was holding tightly to his rib cage.

"I'll call Mum,"

"No Jimmy, please just make me a coffee and go to school."

"No Jack you are in a bloody mess. My Mum needs to help you."

Jack tried to shout at the young man, "No Jimmy," was all he could manage. Jimmy left the couch, put a pot of coffee on and walked out. Within a few minutes he returned with Mary. She was so shocked at the way that Jack looked that she stood in the doorway and put her hand to her mouth. Jimmy went to the coffee pot and poured a steaming mug of coffee, and handed it to Jack. Mary didn't ask any questions. She went to the bathroom and gathered a facecloth and a basin of hot water laced with an antiseptic cleaning solution. Then she proceeded under much protest to clean the cuts and wash the congealed blood from Jack's head and neck. She then went to the bedroom and stripped the bed of all the blood-stained sheets and pillow cases and proceeded to wash them. "Jimmy, please get to school." The boy complied. Mary finally said, "Jack you need to get to a hospital. You are breathing in an odd way. You may have a collapsed lung."

Jack knew she was right. "Can you help me to the car?"

"Yes of course I can," replied Mary. They kept him in overnight and for several more days. Mary thought, *I can't live like this. I have to make other arrangements. I love him but I'm not built to live with this constant fear hanging over us!*

Life quickly returned to normal, Mary at the bakery and Jimmy at school. Mary received a call from the hospital to come and retrieve Jack. He was to be released. Jack looked much better. She got him home; he was still protecting his rib cage on the right side. She made him a pot of coffee and she had prepared a couple of ham and cheese sandwiches, loaded with mayo and mustard, his favourite.

She got home after her shift and made supper for Jimmy, Jack and herself. "Jack, Jimmy and I are going to move out."

"I don't understand Mary?"

"I can't live like this; I've traded one fear for another. I can't stand the thought of you coming home injured again or being found in an alleyway one morning." Mary started to cry.

Jack looked at her and smiled and said, "I think the time is right." She looked at him, incredulous. "I believe you finally love me." She just stared at him and after a long time she nodded in the affirmative. She smiled sweetly at him and thought to herself, *I think I have since the first time I saw you.* "Okay, Mary, here is the deal; there is a golf course that has been asking me to help them sell memberships to well-to-do folk. We won't get rich but at least I can have a steady job in the business that I love and I can still have a little gamble from time to time."

"What do you think?" She got up from the supper table and threw her arms around him and said, "The time is right." Jack's patience finally paid off. He gave up poker and professional gambling or at least she thought he did…

Chapter #17 Who's kidding who?

Jack was taken on to contact influential businessmen, invite them to play golf with him and other businessmen who were already members and encourage them to consider joining the club. This meant paying enormous initiation fees followed by monthly fees to an exclusive golf club. Jack received a small salary, free meals, free golf and a heavy discount on the clothing sold in the pro shop. He always picked out the most outlandish shirts, pants and caps. He became known to the locals as 'the peacock'. In addition to all of those perks and most importantly to Jack he received a large commission on the initiation fee. Jack was a born gambler and he loved the chance to score big for every membership he sold!

He moved Mary and Jimmy into a small rancher near the golf course and she was sure she had never been happier or more blissful. She even planted a small garden with carrots, potatoes, string beans and cabbages. Jack traded the 1958 Dodge Royale for a 1969 Buick Skylark, a convertible that was black with a light interior. Jack brought it home after an exceptional month of selling memberships.

"Jack can we afford this motor car?" asked Mary.

"Mary we don't call them *motor cars* over here in the U.S.," he said in a teasing manner.

"But, can we afford this...car?"

"Oh sure," said Jack but not very convincingly.

The phone rang and Mary picked it up. "Hello."

"Mary it's Shirley, how y'all doing my baby child?"

"Oh Shirley it's great to hear your lovely voice." Once all the niceties were exchanged, Mary asked the question she was almost afraid to ask, "Shirley has anyone come to the ranch asking for me?"

"No, Mary, not a soul, nor has there been any more mail from England except the mail that I've been forwarding to you." Mary breathed a sigh of relief.

"Mary," said Shirley, "how is Jack doing?"

Mary knew what she was asking. "Jack has started coming home later and later. On more than one occasion he has never come home at all." Shirley had seen this pattern many times and she was fearful this behaviour might trigger Jack leaving Mary and Jimmy in the lurch and running off with yet another woman.

"Oh dear, Mary, I'm so sorry to hear that. I think I've warned you many times Jack has always been a womanizer. I believe that you were and you are very special to him but he has a roving eye, and always has."

"What should I do, Shirley?" The long silent pause spoke volumes and Mary closed the awkwardness by saying, "Thank you for phoning Shirley, we love you."

"I love you too child."

Sunday morning came and Jack got up early. Instead of putting on his usual outlandish, colourful golf outfit, he put on one of his pinstripe suits, and very white shirt and a pink and purple patterned tie. *He looked very smart* thought Mary. "Where are you going?"

"To church," answered Jack in an offhanded manner.

"You're going to church? Why?"

"Don't worry you don't have to come. I have a potential client at the golf course that I've been trying to get to buy a membership. He told me that if I went to his church three times that in turn he'll buy a membership. I want the sale and the commission."

"Why does he want you to go to his church?"

Jack smiled at her and said, "I think he wants me to be saved."

"Saved from what?" asked an incredulous Mary.

"You know, saved from myself by being born again."

Mary just looked at him and said, "You mean being religious?"

"Yeah I guess so. I just want the sale and my commission. I'll do whatever I need to, so for the next three Sunday mornings, no golf, I'm going to his church." Mary laughed at the thought of Jack being religious. Sure enough for the next three Sundays, Jack put on a suit and went to church and sure enough the sale was made and his commission was received.

Jimmy got home from school and the house was dark. The curtains were closed and it made him stop as he entered the house. He saw a figure bent over sitting on the couch. He went closer and realised that it was his mother and she was rocking back and forth.

He went to open the curtains and she said "No, please leave them closed."

"Mum, what is the matter?"

"My beautiful Gran has died. I've lost them both now and I'm never going to see them again. I'm never going to sit and have a cup of tea with them". She was inconsolable. Jimmy sat in the dark of the living room with his mother as she grieved her loss and the realization that she was unable to return to her loved ones because of the palpable fear that awaited her return.

Jimmy wondered what to do, "Mum, tell me a story about Gran and Granddad, why where they so special? I'll make a cup of tea for us and you can tell me a story." Mary pulled herself together and thought about what she might tell him this day through the grief.

While still sobbing and sipping her sweet warm tea, she looked at her son and said, "Today is not a time for a story. You were named after him you know."

"Yes I thought I was," responded Jimmy.

Part two

Chapter # 18. The unexpected encounter.

As the guards held him down, she vanished like a vapour. They saw her dark long hair bouncing across her shoulders and down her back as she ran. She was afraid and in shock from the furious slap across the face that almost knocked her off the wooden chair she sat on. The two guards that were standing closest to him raced to the spot and tackled him to the ground, before he could raise another hand to this woman. Three more of her majesty's best prison guards rushed to help their colleagues and it took all five of them to subdue this beast of a man. He was big and bad and most of all he was insane with white hot anger directed at this miserable woman that he'd married. She wasn't his kind of girl at all. She was faint of heart, and she wanted love and family. He wanted loyalty and compliance, someone that could take part in his criminal activities along with him. Why couldn't she just put up and shut up. After all he married her when she was up the stump and no one wanted her, least of all the bloke that got her pregnant.

The big man came by his hardness naturally. He never knew his father, a merchant seaman by all accounts and after a short blissful time with his mother the seaman disappeared and never returned. He was brought up poorly, just surviving on his wits and street smarts as he called it but it was more an unflinching hardness which was his only course of continued existence in the filthy, rat infested streets of East London. His mother was a product of her callous and unloving upbringing; she used sex and pregnancy to trap a man, any man, and a meal ticket. The instant her casual lover learned she was in the family way, he vanished back to a nautical life on the next ship to leave the Victoria docks bound for a life that didn't include this dalliance. Rather than be glad for the new life developing inside of her she hated it and the way it misshaped her body so that men would not look at her in the same way. Now, not only was she unattractive to men she was shunned by the community of the working poor of East London. Some called her loose. Others called her stupid and careless. It didn't matter what words were used she was simple fodder for a world that churned through countless men and women, useful for cleaning, fetching, labouring, lusting. Both she and her son would belong to a class of valueless beings, shackled by no education or knowledge of options, expecting little and getting even less. This was the backdrop of his apprenticeship into the world of thieving, bullying, beating, breaking bones and worse if necessary. None of this mattered to the prison system. The offense was sixty days in solitary confinement, a sentence that could literally drive you mad.

He tried to remember the number of days but they simply melted into each other. Without the telling natural light he lost track of how many times he'd slept and how many days he'd been in the hole and how long before he got out. The darkness was mind numbing and at times he wondered if he would get through this stretch. There had been a few other stints in solitary confinement as the screws called it. This one seemed particularly hard to tolerate.

"Hello, hello," came a voice he wasn't expecting. It was a woman's voice. At first he couldn't process it. *"Am I bleedin' dreaming?"* he thought to himself. "Hello, hello, are you awake?"

"Yes, course I'm awake," was the rough reply. "How did you get in 'ere, and who the bleedin' 'ell are you?"

"Hello my name is Sister Nicola."

He paused, "*A nun*? Piss off, I don't want any religious mumbo jumbo pushed at me. It's bad enough I've got to be in 'ere."

"I've no intention of pushing anything at you, especially not religion. I simply wanted to see if there's anything I can do for you, call a relative, a loved one and let them know how you are doing."

"No! Bugger off and leave me alone." Then the darkness seemed to envelop him as the words left his mouth and he thought better of his harshness toward the voice. "Er, sorry lady, I could use a bit of 'elp alright, what was your name again?" "I'm Sister Nicola, from the Ursuline Convent. What is your name?"

The big man gave his full name as though he was being called before a magistrate. She smiled and said, "How can I help you?"

"It's my trouble and strife. She's done a runner."

"I'm sorry I do not understand your words or what they mean."

"Oh sorry your ladyship, I upset my missus last time she was 'ere and she 'asn't been back. I'd like it if you'd go see 'er and find out 'ow she is and let me know."

"I'd be happy to do that for you. Can you provide me with the address? I shall take it upon myself to travel to your home and have a visit with your wife, and then I'll report back to you as the warden allows."

"Oh ta, I mean yeah, fanks very much your ladyship."

"You must not call me your ladyship. I'm a simple nun. I'm the hands and feet of my Lord and Saviour Jesus Christ. Please just call me Sister or Sister Nicola."

"Er just one more fing Sister, can you spend a few more minutes with me and tell me what's going on in the news."

"Yes of course I can, well at least all that I can remember." The kindly soft spoken sister sat for almost ten uninterrupted minutes with him and spoke of all the news she could think of and he thought how nice it was to hear another human voice, especially a woman's voice. He started to fantasize how he'd like to touch a woman's hair, her skin and smell her perfume. Then he remembered the last nun he saw was on a bus and he thought to himself someone that ugly needed to be hidden away. Then he thought what the voice that was speaking to him through the big steel doors would look like and he shuddered. He thought to himself, "I *know why nuns go into convents, because they are bloody ugly.*" Finally the guard came and told her that her time was up. "I hope to see you soon," were her parting words to him.

****

Sister Nicola stepped off the #9 bus, on Old Ford Road and to her left was the street sign for Monier Road. She soon found number 11. She knocked gently, no answer.

She knocked again and a passerby greeted her, "Ello Sister, the young girl and her boy that used to live 'ere have gone, in the night I suspect, afraid of what 'er so called husband would do to 'er."

"Thank you, do you know where she went?" asked the young pretty nun. "Well someone told me that she 'ad family on the south side of the Thames but that's all I can tell ya."

"Thank you," answered Sister Nicola. "Er, Sister you shouldn't be on this street all by yourself. There are a lot of undesirables around 'ere."

"Thank you sir for your concern, I'm sure I'll be fine." She was standing on Monier Road, on Fish Island.

Fish Island was fifty acres of land in London's east end that was formed by a boundary of water; the river Lea and Union Canal. It was originally procured for a gas works but had become an island of factories and small dingy row houses that the working poor lived in as they provided cheap labour for the different factories.

Sister Nicola looked around and decided to try the tobacconist on the corner. The bell rang as she entered the shop and the man behind the counter was taken aback by the sight of a nun in her habit standing in his shop. "Yes," he *thought how do I address her?* "Hello sir, I'm looking for Mary Yeoman who lived at #11 Monier Road." "Yes she lived here on Fish Island from a teenager. Her husband is doing porridge, so 'er and 'er boy as done a bunk." "Porridge, bunk I'm sorry I don't understand". This was the second time she'd been confronted with cockney slang. "Oh sorry Sister, 'e's gone to jail and she's run off." "Do you know where she went?" "Well, I heard she went to Plumstead on the o'ver side of the Thames but an'over person told me that she'd gone to America, but I dunno for sure." "Thank you for your help." Sister Nicola caught the same series of buses back to the convent and waited for her next scheduled visit to her majesty's prison system to pass on the news.

The weeks passed and the big man never gave the old, ugly nun that spoke to him on the other side of the solid steel door a second thought. He was back in the general population and glad to be so. The junior duty day guard walked past his cell and told him he had a visitor. *"Finally, my missus has come to her senses and come to see me,"* he thought. He was escorted to the visitor day room and there waiting for him was a young and certainly not ugly nun. He sat down across from her and said, "Who are you?" "I'm Sister Nicola of course; we spoke last time I was here and you were in solitary confinement." "You were the one that I spoke to last time?" asked an incredulous inmate.

"Yes of course I was the person. Why are you so surprised?" "Well you're young and you've got a nice boat race..." "Boat race, I don't understand." "Boat race-face, you've got a pretty face." She blushed and looked down, and quickly changed the subject. "I've been to your old neighbourhood and able to find out limited information about the whereabouts of your wife and son." "E's not my son; she was already up the duff when I took 'er in." "Oh I see," said the nun, again she blushed. "It appears that they made their way to south London, Plumstead actually, then perhaps onto America."

"America. Blimey she must have wanted to get away to go that far." His face tensed with a flash of anger but he pretended a smile. Sister Nicola asked if there was anything she could do for him.

"Well, you could come and visit me from time to time. My mover is dead and I 'ave no other family. All my mates don't like coming 'ere."

"I understand, I will come to see you every month. Is there anything you need by way of personal items?"

"Fags can you bring me some fags. I prefer unfiltered cigarettes, Senior Service are the cheapest. I ave a few bob saved up and can pay for the fags."

This time she smiled and said, "Of course I shall bring you your cigarettes, but would you like some reading material, books perhaps?" Before he realized what he was saying he admitted that he couldn't read. One of the most embarrassing things in this man's life was that he couldn't read, not one single word and normally he told no one. And yet in this moment he blurted out his secret to a nun that he didn't even know and he was instantly angry at himself.

"Oh that's no problem why don't I teach you on my monthly visits?"

"Aw, naw I'm too stupid to read, my Mo'ver always said I was too thick to learn anyfink." His honesty touched the young nun's heart and she reached out and touched his hand.

"No one is too stupid to learn to read and I promise you within a few short visits you'll be reading."

He nodded, but didn't really believe her or care. He simply wanted a pipeline to his supply of cigarettes.

Chapter #19 A new creature.

Days passed, and the death of her Nan in England seemed to take a back seat to her worry that Jack Parker was getting ready to leave her and Jimmy and move on to a new woman. He was spending more and more time out in the evening and she was almost positive it meant he'd found another woman. He seemed different in a way she couldn't really comprehend, but she knew something was about to change. She wondered if she could move back to the old bunkhouse that had been her safe place for all those years. After all, she wouldn't be able to pay rent on the house and she'd have to buy another car if Jack left. Then she thought about her job and the safe place it had become. The boss and his wife really liked her and were very good to her, letting her have time off whenever she needed it for Jimmy's school appointments or whatever. Mary wondered what would become of her and her Jimmy, who was now almost six feet tall. The other problem was that he idolized Jack; Jack could do no wrong as far as Jimmy was concerned. By now the boy had a Texas drawl and he worked at sounding like and even acting like his hero Jack. He tried to dress like Jack, wearing loud coloured golf clothes but was made fun of at school so he stopped and returned to his jeans and tee-shirts.

"Mary."
"Yes Jack."
"We need to talk."
"Okay," answered Mary. "Come sit in the living room."
This is it, thought Mary.

"Mary I've been asked to take on the General Manager's job at the golf course. I'll still sell the memberships and get a commission as well as a huge increase in salary."

Mary started to cry, she was expecting to be dumped, told to leave the small rancher they rented, but instead this. The stress had built up and was released and it caused her to break down.

"Mary, why are you crying, are you okay?" asked Jack since this was not the reaction he was expecting at all. Mary tried to speak through her tears and sobs.

"I thought you...were going to tell me...that you were leaving...me."

"What, why on earth were you thinking that?"

"Because you are out many evenings and given your track record with women, I was sure that you were moving on."

Jack looked at her and he smiled and said," I do have a confession to make to you. I have given my life to Christ."

"What," said a bewildered Mary?

"I have become a Christian, and I've been attending bible studies two nights a week, sometimes three."

Mary just looked at him through the tears as if to say *"what on earth are you talking about."*

"Do you remember when the client I'd been trying to sell a membership to told me if I attended three services at his church, he'd buy a membership?"

"Yes, I do," answered a still bewildered Mary.

"Well at the first service the minister spoke about Christ dying to cover my sins and as you know Mary I have more than most." Jack was trying to inject a little humour into the moment. "Then he said that He, Christ, would have died just to cover my sins which would make me clean before God and that I would be a new creature in Christ. It would mean a new start for an old reprobate like me. All that week the thought of my many dreadful sins being washed away and me being given a brand-new start seemed too good to be true, but it kept playing over and over in my mind. It even woke me up in the middle of the night. So, on the following Sunday, I was on the fence whether I'd go back but I did and the minister talked about Heaven and hell and that the people that accepted Christ as their personal Saviour were going to Heaven. I didn't know what that meant but then he said that Jesus was waiting to speak to me and that all I had to do was invite him into my life, tell him I was a sinner and ask Him to help me and take control of my life. Then he asked if there was anyone that wanted that assurance and I've never wanted anything more, so I jumped up and almost ran to the front...I'm a Christian, and I've never felt a peace like this in my life. Then only weeks later I'm asked to become the General Manager of the golf course. It's a God thing Mary. It's got to be, me Jack Parker Jr, gambler, philanderer, untrustworthy, the guy voted most likely not to succeed, a General Manager."

Mary was so dumbfounded that she just sat there with her mouth open and stared at Jack.

Mary didn't know how to process this news and so she didn't. She was just happy Jack was not turning her and her son out into the street and she really loved Jack. Jack bought Jimmy his first set of golf clubs that had been traded in by a well-to-do businessman at the club.

"Jimmy my club pro is going to give you a lesson or two. Plus we have junior tournaments on Thursday afternoons during the school holidays. You might want to try your hand at golf. If you'd like, I'll get you a job as a caddy at the club. You'll make some money and the tips can be very good."

Jimmy agreed without hesitation, he could spend more time with his hero. Jimmy took his new set of used clubs to the driving range to give them a try. *Nothing to this golf,* he thought, *I've seen old men on Shells Wonderful World of Golf on TV, and if they can do it I'm sure I'll be able to.* He hit two large buckets of balls and never hit one straight; he was drenched in sweat and frustration. Jack was watching from the Manager's office and saw just how bad Jimmy was at this game he loved.

"Jimmy, you can't just pick up a club and be good at golf. It's a very difficult game to learn but you are tall and thin. I'd refer to you as a good looking flat-belly and flat-belly's can golf. I think you're going to be great at this game." Young Jimmy beamed from ear to ear and rode home with Jack determined to get good at golf no matter what it took.

Chapter #20 Noddy in Toyland

Sister Nicola came to the prison as she promised every month; she was permitted to spend one half hour with the big man, no more. On the first two visits he feigned interest in learning the alphabet, but his real motive was the fags. He really wanted to keep Sister Nicola bringing his cigarettes, since his wife had disappeared without a trace. He burned with white anger when he thought about her. Cigarettes were the currency of the jail; a man could get a lot of things done on the outside with a constant supply of cigarettes. The young nun battled through his indifference and smiled sweetly at this man that occasionally took the Lord's name in vain which tore at her soul.

On the third visit after another slip she couldn't take it anymore and called him by his full name and said, "If you continue to take the Lord's name in vain, I shall have to stop these visits."

He was so shocked at being told off for swearing by this little, pretty nun, he smiled and said, "Er I'm sorry, I'll make a real effort to stop Sister, really I will." She went back to his lesson. At the end of the time together, she handed him a book. It was a child's book called Noddy Goes to Toyland.

He looked at the book and looked at her and said, "What do you want me to do w'th this?"

"Try to make out very simple words. Try to sound them out like I showed you and on my next visit we'll read it together."

"You must be bleedin joking, ain't ya, do you know how much these blokes in 'ere will take the piss out of me?" He paused and realized he swore again but he was incredulous.

She was hurt and didn't understand.

"I'm sorry for swearing but if the blokes in here see me reading this, I'll be a laughing stock."

"It's the simplest book I know of, " insisted the nun. "Please at least try." He quickly shoved the book inside his prison jacket between his arm and his ribs hoping that none of the other inmates saw the exchange. The old guard that escorted him back to his cell smirked and said quietly "Noddy goes to Toyland" as he closed the cell door. The big man realized that Sister Nicola would have to declare the book and papers being brought into prison for his reading lesson. He hoped that the jailers wouldn't breathe a word of it to the other inmates. He wouldn't have long to find out. The big man was ushered down along with the other inmates on his cell block as usual for the early meal of the day. While standing in the long line for his food he heard a loud conversation somewhere in the line up for breakfast behind him.

"So what are you going to do after breakfast? I think I'll go back to my cell and read Noddy Goes to Toyland." Laughter erupted throughout the mess hall. He stood frozen and his face was turning blood red, whether from embarrassment or anger, it didn't matter.

He turned very slowly and announced at the top of his voice, "I'm learning to read. If anyone has a ruck with me reading any book, they should be man enough to tell me to my face in the exercise yard." He received no takers. The inmates kept their collective heads down; most didn't want trouble with the beast. He was big, he had a barrel chest and he sported a very black beard to hide the complexion that was scarred from a hideous case of acne from years of improper personal hygiene. His eyes were black with permanent big black circles that seemed to continue across his cheeks. The guards ran to the spot in the food line where he was getting his breakfast, but the crisis passed without further incident.

He didn't know why but he was looking forward to her next visit. She arrived as promptly as always and they went over the book together. She was overly impressed with how many words he had understood himself and they read and re-read the book that had caused so much embarrassment.

As the visit came to an end, she looked at him and said, "I hope you don't mind me saying but your mother was wrong. You are anything but thick-headed. In fact, I perceive you to be as bright as a whip and a quick study. You'll be reading in no time at all." He beamed from ear to ear and she realized that was the first time she'd ever seen any evidence of pure happiness in this poor man's life.

"Why 'ave you kept coming to see me? You know what I am. I'm a criminal, always 'ave been, always will be."

She took a deep breath and said, "I took an oath to help people. When I was just starting my life of service in the convent I asked who should I help. I was told to go into the world and put one foot in front of the other and that God would show me who needed his help and love."

"Aw, I ain't got time for God. He's never 'elped me. All I ever got when I asked for 'elp was a swift kick up the trousers, if you know what I mean. If there is a God, he don't want me."

"Have you ever directly spoken to him and asked him for help?"

"Are you barmy? I can't speak to God. He don't ave anyfink to do w'th the likes of me!"

"You are so mixed up, don't you think we are all sinners, not just you. I'm a sinner. I sin every day, and everyone does."

"Na not you sister, you are the closest thing I ever met to being perfect."

She smiled and said, "Do you think that God keeps a record of sins and grades them into marginal sins, and worst sins and really bad sins, no he does not! A sin is a sin whether you've stolen an item or as in my case when I commit a sin of selfishness of thought. It's all the same to God."

"Oye, w'th all due respect I told you in the beginning that I didn't want any religious mumbo jumbo, didn't I?"

"Yes, you did but with all due respect to you, what I'm telling you has nothing to do with religion and everything to do with a loving God that wants you to turn to him for help and forgiveness. Nothing more and nothing less...not religion! Now let's get on with reading this book and when you have finished it I'll bring another that will not cause you as much embarrassment." She smiled at him so sweetly that he realised just how beautiful this nun was. He counted the days until the next visit and as it got closer he was unusually happy especially the day of her visit.

He had a permanent smile plastered to his face which was noticed by his fellow inmates and even the guards. "Oye you seem an 'appy man today. As it got anyfink to do with the fact that that young nun is coming to teach you to read? She's not interested in you, ya great pillock, she's after saving your soul for Jesus," the guard taunted and then laughed. At the appointed time looking like a cross between a penguin and an angel she arrived carrying two books and a sweet smile. The big man sat at the wooden table that was ablaze in scratches of words and pictures, some inappropriate and some worse. They both ignored the grotesque sexual messages that adorned the big oak table. They shook hands as usual and this time the big, dark man held on to her milky white hand for a long time until in confusion she pulled it away.

"I'm very glad you came to teach me today, I've been looking forward to it."

"Good," she remarked in a matter of fact manner and opened the same book; they had read for the past two visits.

"I thought we was gonna read from a different book. I'm getting tired of Noddy Goes to Toyland," he said in a mocking manner.

"Be patient we will move on to another book when you are ready. Can you trust me?"

"Course," he said in a disappointing way. "Ere, did you bring me any fags?"

"Yes, of course, as usual. Now let's read together." This exercise went on for months and she was completely taken aback at how well he had learned to read and so was he. They visited every month and discussed each and every book. To her surprise he read some of the books several times and seemed to comprehend more than she would have believed.

"He is a good student," she bragged to Mother Superior at the Ursuline Convent.

Mother Superior smiled at her knowingly and said, "Be careful not to get to close emotionally to him because when his sentence is up he'll go back to his outside life and it stands to reason it will not include you and your teaching."

"Thank you, Mother, I'm sure you are right but at least he'll go back to his life with another life skill that may help him to turn his life away from criminality."

"Very true my child, very true."

Chapter #21 I'm still here

After five years at Wormwoods Scrubs certain inmates could feel if there was something in the air and the big man knew that something was going on.

George Blake was imprisoned at 'The Scrubs' for forty-two years as a double agent, working for MI6. He was in truth a KGB spy, and totally committed to the communist system, after experiencing the bombing of North Korea by the west many years before.

The forty-two-year sentence seemed harsh but not compared to P.S. Popov who it turned out was, like Blake, a British double agent working inside the GRU. Blake exposed him and he was subsequently executed in 1960. During Blake's double agent era he exposed over forty western spies many of whom were executed or disposed of in some manner.

During his first few years in jail Blake got in tight with a couple of anti-nuclear campaigners, Michael Randle and Pat Pottle. An escape plan was hatched by another of their pals, Sean Bourke. Bourke was sentenced to seven years for sending a letter bomb through the British post office to a detective at Scotland Yard. Once outside he worked with the anti-nuclear men Michael Randle and his friend Pottle to get the double agent out of Wormwood Scrubs and back to the Soviet Union.

The big man was in the exercise yard walking around the walking track as they all were required to do, silently. He saw George Blake walking towards him. This he thought was unusual. His kind always kept to themselves. There is a class system even in prison; educated people like Blake would never be caught speaking with the likes of the big man, a common thug, a career criminal. Blake's transgressions were based on principle, while the common criminals were sordid and ignoble. It disgusted Blake.

As he passed the beast he said, "Excuse me. My name is George Blake."

"I know exactly who you are and what you've done." He wanted to call him a few more names laced with some threatening language. In fact, he would have loved nothing more than to grab Blake, push him against the brick wall and do a number on his face for Queen and country. But he remembered the last time he was in solitary and didn't want to return.

The next time they passed each other, he said, "What do you want, you disgusting commie." Blake was afraid but he needed some muscle to help him escape, especially once he got outside. He needed the protection of a man like this one, one that knew his way around the dark alleys and dangerous places.

"I'm breaking out and I need someone to come with me," said a nervous Blake. He'd served in the British Navy, and come across many a hard man but this big and dark man was frightening even to other criminal inmates. Blake was at heart an academic, with values and immoveable belief of right and wrong and while he believed he was on the side of right, he was very afraid of this fearsome behemoth of a man. Blake was born in Holland to Dutch mother and a Jewish father. The family name was Behar but they legally changed it to Blake after moving to England.

On the next pass, "What makes you fink I'd help a bleedin' traitor to England like you?" Even his voice was flat and ominous.

"For money and a way out of here, I know you still have two years to serve." He was correct the big man chaffed at the thought of another two years of confinement.

"Ow much money is we talking about?"

"It's enough money to set you and your family up for the rest of your life."

"I don't 'ave a family anymore. She buggered off to America". On the next pass, "I'll fink about it," he said sternly.

The money was enticing but getting out was the real hook, and he was going to put his disgust aside for this communist spy and use him to get the money but most importantly, freedom. If this Blake did have a plan to break out of 'the Scrubs' he wanted in on it! They whispered small snippets of information as Blake walked slowly around the exercise yard. He'd pass the beast and give him times, location, when he'd receive the money and then finally the actual date. Blake's long years in the dark world of espionage conditioned him to only give out enough information to get to the next step and nothing more. In return he was to arrange for several safe houses and to move himself and Blake every two days. Above all he had to protect him. After all he was one of the most reviled men in England. He also had to arrange for safe passage out of England to the continent and from there the KGB would take over and get him and all of his information to Lubyanka Square in Moscow and safety.

"Alright, I'm in," said the beast, "When?"

"A week from this coming Saturday," whispered Blake as they passed each other in the yard.

Two days later was the monthly visit from Sister Nicola. He was trying to concentrate on reading but his mind kept wandering to the escape plan and he kept losing his place.

"What's wrong?" asked the Sister.

"Nofink," was the reply but he wouldn't look at her.

She bowed her head and then looked up at his dark eyes in a playful manner and said, "Is something bothering my best pupil?"

"I'm getting out of 'ere. I've 'ad enough of this bloody place. I got a chance to escape and I'm taking it," he quietly blurted out.

"But you've only got two years to go. If you are caught you'll have to start all over again. This is insane."

"Alright keep your voice down," said the big man. She just looked at him and big tears appeared in the corner of her eyes and ran down her cheeks. He was stunned and completely lost for words.

"I...I gotta get out of 'ere, this is a good chance." He didn't know what else to say.

"Are you going to grass me up to the screws?"

"If you're asking me if I'm going to tell anyone you don't know me at all." She stood up and looked down at him sitting in the chair, his head was down. "I thought you were a clever man caught up in a socially impoverished world that didn't value good decision making or reasoning. You will be caught, maybe soon, maybe later, but you will be caught. Then you will receive another long prison term and be back in this cesspool of an institution, like an animal in a cage. That will be your lot in life, and you are so much better than that. You can make something of yourself but only if you make better decisions." Sister Nicola turned and left him sitting there, alone and wondering what just happened. He would never stand to be spoken to by any man like he was by this nun. He would have struck a man down in a heartbeat. The only thought that crossed his mind was, *"I hope she comes back."* He desperately wanted her to, but she didn't and eventually he was escorted back to his cell.

On Saturday October 22, 1966 Blake broke a window at the end of the hallway where his cell was located. Then between six and seven pm, while the other inmates and guards were watching the weekly movie, Blake simply climbed out of the window, slid down the roof of a porch and got to the perimeter wall. Waiting for him was a homemade rope ladder onto which he climbed over the walls of the famous Wormwood Scrubs prison as per his plan. He was shuttled from safe house to safe house until he found passage to the continent and to the safety of Russia. The big man was a 'no show.'

At the breakfast table one cold December morning, Mother Superior announced to the group of nuns that some of them had items in post. Much to Sister Nicola's surprise she had a letter. She didn't recognize the hand writing, or the postmark. She opened the envelope and inside she found a piece of paper with words cut out from a newspaper and glued together on the page. It simply read, *I'm still here!*

On the next available visiting day she made plans to visit the Scrubs. The guard told him he had a visitor, he knew it was her. He was delighted and tickled pink, like a little boy that had found a place of light in his life. He bounced off the grey lumpy mattress that rested on a steel cot and looked in the mirror to see if he was presentable. He ran his fingers through his dark hair several times and pushed his shirt down the inside front of his prison issued trousers and synched his belt a little tighter and made his way to the visitor hall. He walked through the doors and saw her sitting there looking off to the only window in the visitor's hall and at that moment he knew. For the first time in his existence he encountered what love was.

The months that followed were routine. The visits always meant a new book or two. He was reading at a very good level. He loved the mysteries and a few of the Western books she was able to find. During one of the visits she presented him with a piece of paper with lines on it and a capital 'A' in the top left and a non-capital 'a'. "I want you to write these two letters out as many times as you can on this paper."

"I can't write. You know I can't," he said incredulous.

"Yes I know but before your confinement is over you will." She smiled that smile that he was unable to resist.

"All right then, I'll try."

"Only seventeen more visits and you my favourite and only pupil will be a free man. If I have my way you be a free man that can read and write." He smiled at the thought of it and then took a long draw on his cigarette.

Not many of his old contacts visited him; most of them were criminals and were naturally not comfortable voluntarily walking into a prison. One or two occasionally made the trip to 'The Scrubs'. "Ere, what you gonna do when your porridge is over?"

"Get back out on the Rob of course. 'Ow else am I going to get by?" said the large man.

"Where you gonna live though? Where are you gonna go? You've got no gaff. Will you go to America to git your old lady back?"

"Naw she's gone and I'm well shot of 'er. I'm glad to be rid of 'er. She was afraid of her own shadow."

"Does the nun still bring you fags every visit?"

"Yeah, she does so, what of it?"

"Nofink, you just seem different than you were before."

"What do you mean different?"

"I dunno, just different."

"Don't talk out of your arse," which was his way of saying that part of the conversation was at an end. On the wall of his cell was a calendar of sorts. It was really a countdown of weeks and months, only 6 more before he was to be released back onto the callous streets of London.

He thought about what he'd do and where he'd go and he was puzzled. Part of him was excited to get back into his old life but he knew that somewhere in a place inside of him that was unfamiliar that she'd have nothing to do with him anymore once he started back into the underworld. He was conflicted; would he choose making a living in the old way or having his life intertwined with his nun.

****

Finally, the day had arrived and he was hoping she'd be there. He remembered the day so long ago when his wife, he could hardly remember what she looked like now, ran out. He was taken and held down by the guards. He was glad now that they did. He was so livid he really thought he could have killed her. Then he tried to remember the last time he got really angry, he couldn't. He got to the big doors; his heart was pounding in his chest. The duty guard handed him a ten shilling note and a bus pass. They had supplied him a brown pin stripe suit, that didn't fit very well, a grey shirt that was white once and a brown and beige tie. He wondered who had worn these clothes before him. He opened the smaller door which was cut out of the huge oak castle-like doors and stepped out. He'd dreamed about this moment, over and over again. For seven years he'd been told every minute when to sleep, eat and every other possible direction was provided. Now he was confused, not afraid but confused, where would he go? What would he do? The real moment of decision was here and he was alone. Just as that thought washed over him, an arm threaded through his and he turned to see his penguin, with the biggest smile he'd ever seen on her pretty face.

"I'm here Timothy Green, I'm here." They rode the bus back to the convent; she wanted Mother Superior and the other sisters to meet him. She had arranged for a bedsit room not far from the convent. She had visited businesses and two firms had told her that they would consider the convict for a position working in a factory setting.

Timothy Green stood in the dining room of the small convent and he was trembling. He was overwhelmed at the thought that he was standing in this building waiting for; *some old girl they called Mo'ver Superior, some old lady looking down er nose at him just like they have his whole life...what am I doing ere? I should be looking for my old mates and get a few good pints of best bitter down my neck. This is a joke.*

Just then the love of his life entered the dining room with another penguin, older but kindly and she reached out and took his hand in both of hers and said, "Welcome Timothy, I've heard so much about you and what a nice chap you are."

He was set back on his heels. "Oh Ta, fank you very much Mo'ver."

"Would you like a cup of tea and some jam cake, Timothy?"

"*Oh yeah, Ta,*" said the big man still clutching his prison issued duffle bag. They sat there drinking tea and eating cake.

"I understand you are a fine student of Sister Nicola's. She brags about how quickly you learn."

"Na, I fink she is just a good teacher, at's all. Er this cake ain't half bad, can I pinch another bit?"

"Of course, please help yourself," said the kindly old Mother Superior. He finished a third piece of cake and leaned back in his chair.

"Is it alright if I smoke?"

Sister Nicola, went to protest, but the Mother, touched her hand and smiled and said, "Yes of course, let me find you something to use as an ashtray." She found lid of a jar and he puffed away.

Sister Nicola and Timothy Green walked the few blocks to the bedsit that she'd arranged for him. "Timothy, I've been thinking perhaps we might continue to have a reading and writing lesson weekly. We can have it the library at the convent. What do you say to that?"

"Aye, sure whatever you say Sister." She didn't get the feeling he was as enthusiastic as he was in prison to carry on with the lessons.

"If you'd rather not continue with the lessons and just go on your way that's fine too".

"No, no I want to see you every week, er for the reading and writing lesson for sure," he recovered quickly.

"Remember you have an appointment tomorrow at the paint factory at ten a.m. and at the Coop floor mill at two in the afternoon." He grunted at her but had no intention of attending either of those interviews.

As soon as she left he headed to the nearest pub and purchased as much best bitter as his ten-shilling note afforded him. The next morning, he woke up with that long forgotten memory of being just a little hungover and very hungry. He didn't have enough for a full breakfast or even a bacon buttie. He looked at the clock and realized that if he got ready quickly he could still make it to the ten o'clock interview at Pinchin & Johnson's paint factory. It was located on Silvertown Way, in Canningtown, East London. It was a huge brick factory. Since he had no money for the bus he walked and made it just in time.

He approached the security guard at the factory gate. "Oye, I'm 'ere for the ten o'clock interview for a job." The old fellow in the guard hut thought he was a little disrespectful but didn't say anything due to his size and menacing look. He called the office and after a few minutes a man in white overalls came to the gate and collected Timothy Green for his interview.

"My name is Ernie Murphy and I'm the shop foreman. The job is simply filling forty-five-gallon barrels from three thousand gallon mixing tanks and then rolling the filled barrels onto a wooden flat which are picked up by the forklift. It's hard, dirty work. Are you up to it?"

"Yeah, I suppose I am. Look I'm just out of the prison system and I can start work as soon as you like but I'll need a sub on my wages. I haven't eaten today and I have no money for bus fare".

Ernie stood up and said, "Come with me."

Timothy thought he was going to throw him out. Instead he took him to the cafeteria, which was a huge room that could seat hundreds of people. It reminded Timothy of the prison cafeteria, and he didn't like it.

Ernie took him to the front and said to the gal working behind the counter, "Give this chap whatever he'd like to eat and put it on my ticket."

"Timothy, take your time I'll come back for you in twenty minutes and we'll get you sorted out with some overalls and enough money for bus fare and food for the rest of the week." The big man was flabbergasted.

Ernie walked away and Timothy called out after him, "Er why are you elping me?"

"I'm elping you because many years ago Mother Superior helped me in the same way. I'll see you in twenty minutes."

Chapter #22 Impossible

"Shirley, Jack told me that he has become a Christian," Mary excitedly proclaimed.

The phone went dead. "What did you say child?" inquired Shirley thinking that her hearing was leaving her.

"Jack announced to me that he has become a Christian. What does that mean?" said Mary.

"Mary, I'm dumbstruck, I never thought I'd hear the words Jack and Christian in the same sentence." Mary smiled. She loved the way that Shirley had such cute sayings that seemed to sum up the situation perfectly. "I'm not really sure what it means. I've had a few acquaintances over the years that called themselves Christians, but they were a little kook-a-looey if you know what I mean?"

"He goes to bible study too, sometimes three times a week, at night."

"Mary are you sure he not seeing someone and using this as his alibi?" Shirley felt bad saying that to Mary as soon as it came out but it just came out without too much thought.

The phone went dead from the other side. "No Shirley I really don't think so. He seems to have really changed. I can't explain it, but he is different".

"Mary, give me an example of what you mean changed."

"Well he's kinder, more thoughtful and much less demanding. Two days ago, he brought me a cup of coffee while I was still in my bed. He has never done anything like that before."

"You are right my sweet girl, that does not sound like the Jack Parker I know. I think I'd better have a chat with Reverend Duet at the Episcopalian church, you remember the man that did my Jed's funeral. He'll give me some answers to my questions and I'll call you again."

"Okay, Shirley, I love you."

"I love you too child." The phone went dead. Mary hung the phone back on its cradle and felt unsure for her role with Jack and his newfound faith. A few days later Jimmy was hovering around his mother. She knew from experience that he wanted to tell her something.

"Mum?"

"Yes, Jimmy."

"Do you believe in Jesus?"

"Yes of course I do. Remember when you were a little boy back in England we'd go to church at Christmas and Easter and pray to Jesus." He nodded, "But if we do believe in Jesus why do we only go to church and pray to him a few times a year?"

"Has Jack been speaking to you about God stuff?"

"Well kinda, he wants me to try going to the youth group at his church."

"Do you want to?"

"I really don't know but I do want to please Jack. I wish he was my real Dad." His mother smiled and wondered where this 'born again' business would end. Jimmy was still a slightly below average student, but he had become a slightly better than average golfer. He was at the driving range as often as he could be. He'd play until it was well past dark. Many times, he'd participate in a putting for dimes contest with whoever would take him on. Sometimes he would be putting in complete darkness aided by the light of the clubhouse window. He was an awesome putter. He had an uncanny knack of being able to see the line and his confidence grew. Jack loved to coach him and he took credit for Jimmy's growing prowess on the links. He caddied most weekends and in the beginning, he was shy and hardly spoke other than the odd, "Yes sir".

Local golfers treated him well since the General Manager was his father or at least that was what they thought. As Jimmy's putting legend grew, golfers old and young would approach him and ask them to show them how he was able to sink so many putts. His confidence was growing. He was finding it easier to speak with people particularly about golf. They listened to him and they didn't see him as that beige boy at all.

"Jimmy, have you considered being a golf professional?" asked Jack.

"You mean on the tour?" asked a naïve Jimmy.

Jack smiled and said, "No not on the tour. You're good but you're not at the level. I was thinking as a teaching pro, or a club pro, it's a good life. You won't get rich but it's a great life and one day you might grow into being a GM just like yours truly." Jack did a little jig, right there in the pro shop. Jimmy laughed and pushed into his hero and the two just smiled at each other. Jack put his arm around the boy and the two marched out together.

"C'mon lad of mine I'm fixin to get you home for some nourishment. Besides it's getting dark." Jack was always joking around. Members always wanted to be on the right side of the General Manager, for special favors like ideal tee-times and discounts on items in the pro shop. Jack had become the consummate GM. His sense of humor was legendary. It was second only to his ability to have people owe him favors and he used those favours to ingratiate himself with the real movers and shakers in the Louisiana golf community. Jack's standing in the golf world was growing.

****

"Reverend Duet, I have a nephew that claims to have become a born-again Christian."

"I see," said the old man. He was on his guard; since he'd lost more than a few of his flock to those fire and brimstone preachers that had something that he didn't seem to possess, passion and charisma. While he didn't have it, he had a grudging respect for those that did.

"I've seen a number of people that have left the mainline churches like ours and joined other, shall I say, more charismatic organizations. The bottom line is that if it brings him into a God-believing church, it's got to be a good thing."

"Yeah I suppose so. It's just that he's always been such a rascal and now this. I just would never have believed it."

"Shirley you need to embrace it. I've long since stopped concerning myself with what church a man attends as long as he is attending somewhere, and he has faith in something other than himself." As he spoke those words he couldn't help thinking that he wasn't being entirely truthful. He hated losing parishioners to another church. It made him feel like he'd failed. His long years and perhaps the hot Texas sun had made him take the high road in most things, but in his heart, it still bothered him.

Shirley hugged the old Reverend and jumped into the pick-up and headed for the HEB grocery store to get a few things and contemplated about what the Reverend Duet said. But it just didn't sit right with her, Jack Parker and church...impossible!

"Hey Jack."

"Howdy Ben," said Jack to the backshop head caddie. "You might want to keep your eye on your son Jimmy. He's spending time with the Kirby brothers and I've been smelling alcohol on his breath a few times. I think he might be drinking a little and he is still pretty young for that."

"Thanks Ben I will." Ben was an old-time caddie, black and poor but with a heart of gold. He had raised a family of five on a caddie's wages and his wife Maisel's cleaning job at the hospital. Jack was more than a little rattled; Jimmy had been a good boy all the years he'd known him. He had seen more than one good man brought down by drinking. On the way home from the golf course Jack started the conversation.

"How was your day Jimmy?"

"Fine. I shot a seventy-eight from the blue tees. I kicked arse in that foursome".

"Good. Did you have any alcohol to help you?"

Jimmy's head jerked sideways toward Jack, "How did you know?"

"I know everything, and I also know it was not your first time. Stay away from the Kirby brothers. They are trouble."

"Are you going to tell my Mum?"

"Not unless I catch you at it again…Okay?"

"It's a deal I won't drink again and you don't tell my mum."

"Okay," said Jack as seriously as he could muster. They went on to talk about Jimmy's round of seventy-eight that day and Jack asked him to explain why he was six strokes over par. The feeling was that Jack wanted and expected better while Jimmy was more than pleased with a seventy-eight, especially from the longer blue tees.

Two weeks went by and Jack all but forgot about the Kirby brothers and Jimmy's drinking. Ben poked his head into Jack's office off the pro shop and looked frightened.

"Jack, we got a serious problem, you'd better come." Jack slowly got up and followed Ben into the caddie's area behind the bag shop where they kept the member's golf bags.

Jimmy was passed out on the floor in a fetal position. "Jimmy. C'mon son let's go."

"He's not sleeping Jack; I've tried waking him he's...he's'."

"It's alright Ben, I know what he is. He is drunk. I'll take care of it. I'm sorry this has landed on your watch."

"No problem boss, don't worry no one knows about it and they won't hear anything from me."

"Thank you Ben." Jack got him to the car and he slumped in the back seat.

On the way home Jimmy said, "Jack the car is spinning," and then proceeded to throw up all over the back seat and the floor mats.

Mary watched Jack carry him into the house and deposit him on his bed and Jack simply said. "He is drunk."

Mary was quick to lay blame, "Who would have given my boy liquor?"

"Mary I hate to have to say this to you but this isn't the first time. He's been hanging around with the Kirby brothers. Old man Kirby is well known for makin White Lightening."

"What?"

"White Lightening Mary, it's alcohol, moonshine, homemade liquor."

"You've known about this?"

"Yes I've caught him before but he promised me that if I didn't tell you he'd stop."

"You should have told me."

"I know but I thought it was a teenage thing. Most kids try it one time. It seems to be a rite of passage here in the states."

"What am I going to do? What are we going to do? He wishes you'd be his father you know."

Jack, stood there and said, "Yeah I know. I think a lot of him too, but not at this very moment. Mary, I'm going to pray for Jimmy." As they stood there Jack closed his eyes and started praying. "Father, Lord Jesus I'm not sure what to pray but Jimmy is in trouble. He is drinking and we are very worried about him. Can you help us? Amen."

Mary just stood there shocked and wide eyed.

"What's the matter Mary?" "I've never seen anyone do that before."

"What?" "Pray out loud, it seemed like a strange thing to do."

"Really," said Jack "only if you don't believe that God exists. If you believe that God is real and he is there for you, why wouldn't you talk to him? Why wouldn't you ask him to help us?"

"I don't know why," she was uncomfortable and immediately left the room.

Later that night the bedroom door opened and out came Jimmy, his eyes on the ground and head down from embarrassment and shame.

"Okay young man, come and sit down right here," said Mary.

"Mum, I'm sorry I won't do it again. I promise."

"Drinking, drinking!" she raised her voice and sounded excited and shrill. Jack sat there and thought to himself, *I've never seen her in this state before, she must be very worried.* "You must stop this drinking immediately, do you understand?" she was frantic. Jack just watched, and was confused. This gal who was usually quiet and unassuming was going at her son like he'd never seen before and she was bordering on being emotionally out of control.

To cut the tension, Jack said "Jimmy you must be hungry. Why don't you go to the kitchen and make yourself a sandwich?"

As he left Jack said, "Mary what has gotten into you? I know this is a serious issue but you are about to lose it."

"Shut up Jack, and stay out of this. I will not let this happen again." Jack was hurt and shocked at her telling him to shut up; he jumped in his car and went to the office to cool off.

The next morning over coffee, he asked her the question that had been burning in his mind. "Mary, what did you mean, I won't let this happen again?"

"Never mind Jack, I'm sorry that I told you to shut up."

"I got to say that one stung a little. Please tell me what you mean that you won't let this happen again."

"Jack I love you, please let it go." He wasn't going to.

"Look, if there is something in the past that I should know about please tell me."

"No Jack, I will not talk about it ever. I'm going to work." Mary left Jack sitting at the table; he was feeling decidedly left out of this piece of the family history.

Weeks went by and Jack almost forgot about the drinking incident, but the way she reacted and the slip she made about "it's not happening again" would not leave him.

Jack waited for a couple of days and while Jimmy was at the golf course, caddying one Saturday morning he made coffee and took it into her while she was in bed. She rubbed her eyes and sat up in appreciation for the gesture of him bringing her coffee in bed. "Mary, I need you to tell me what you meant when you said I won't let this happen again. It's been bothering me for days and I can't get it out of my head."

Mary paused and thought how to tell this story. She patted the bed and said, "Come sit here with me. I'll tell you the story, but I warn you it's not pretty. You might see me in a different light after you hear what I tell you."

"When I was seventeen, the factory that I worked at in London was owned and run by a family that had a several children. One of them was a young man whose name was James, not Jim or Jimmy. The family insisted that he was called James especially by us workers. He treated me sweetly and eventually we went out together. I soon realized that he was unable to handle his drink; he got completely drunk every time we went out. I mean completely. It seemed that he couldn't stop once he started. Eventually I noticed that he was drinking at work. He smelled of drink during the day. He asked me to marry him and spoke of love and fidelity. I worried about the drinking, but I hoped it would pass. I became pregnant, and after I told him I never saw him again from that moment on. Several days later I was sacked on the spot on the shop floor. I asked the family where he was and was told that he was sent to a private hospital. They told me that I wasn't good enough for their son, that I was riff raff." She cried when she retold that story even though it had been many years in the past, the pain and embarrassment was still very real. "I went off and soon after met the man that took me in even though I was pregnant, Timothy Green. He said he didn't care that I was pregnant and wanted to marry me right away to cover up what had happened. I didn't know him very well. We met in a pub and my friend told him that I was in the family way. Even though he knew, he was nice to me and he seemed like a way out of a very frightening circumstance that I'd gotten myself into. Sadly, it wasn't until after I married him that I found out I had married a violent criminal. My life spiraled down from that point on until I was sent to Texas for my protection."

Jack moved closer to her and took her in his arms and told her that she was the second best thing that ever happened to him, after Jesus. She confessed to Jack that she was terrified that Jimmy would turn out just like his father with the drink. Jack agreed that seemed to be the case and now he understood why she'd reacted frenetically when Jimmy kept getting involved with alcohol. "I'm glad you told me Mary. It explains your reactions to the recent events." He winked at her, and kissed her on the cheek.

Chapter #23 back to the Rob

Weeks had gone by and Timothy Green had filled hundreds of forty-five-gallon steel barrels of paint. The empty barrels sat on a steel frame in front of a three thousand gallon mixing tank. His repetitive job was to lift the cock on the tank, watch the paint pour into the barrel until it was almost full and then take a steel wrench and close the stop on the barrel. Then he would roll it off the frame and onto the wooden pallet. When the pallet was full the forklift would carry it off and bring him a new pallet and he'd start over again. He lived for his weekly reading and writing lesson with Sister Nicola, but really it was just being near her. At times he wanted to tell her that he was hopelessly in love with her, but he was afraid that she would stop the lessons. After all what would a lovely, young attractive person want with a huge giant of a man, with a horrible pockmarked face and significant criminal record...*nofink of course!*

Six weeks into the job on a Friday morning the big man was summoned to the union office.

The union man was named Alf Whitehead, and he didn't mince his words. "Tim, we want you to be a shop steward of the paint fillers shop."

"Why me I've only been doing this for a few weeks? I'm not sure I'm staying anyway."

"It's simple my man, the others are afraid of you, all of them."

"So what?" he responded.

"Timothy Green," said the union man as he leaned into to him, "We want shop stewards that can get the rank and file to vote the way that we want them to. Here's how it works; the voting is a simple show of hands, and you make sure that your people in your shop sit behind you in the cafeteria in a group. When we call for a show of hands on a vote we tell you what we want, and you tell them. When the vote is called for, you turn and face them and if anyone votes against what we want, you just scowl at them. If they continue against us, you will have to 'ave a little chat with them, if you know what I mean?"

"Course I know what you mean, what's in it for me?"

"Timothy mate, there's lots in it for you. You'll get an additional eighty-five shillings a week paid by the union." Timothy quickly did the reckoning and realized that eighty-five shillings was four pounds and five shillings.

"You decide who works on what job. You and I know that all jobs are dirty but some are far worse than others. You make sure you get the best, easiest jobs. You get two hours a day to work on union business. That's time you don't have to fill barrels, what do you say? I'd think you could keep that lot of buggers in the filling shop in line. After all they are the scum of the earth. Most of them are stupid; in fact, most of them are bleedin' foreigners that are thick as bloody posts anyway. What do you say?"

Timothy stood up and put his face close to Alf Whitehead's and said, "I do not like you mate." Alf drew back in fear; it wasn't what he was expecting.

"I'll talk to you after the weekend. That's when I'll give you my answer!" He walked out and went back to his job filling barrels.

On his way home that Friday night he stopped into a pub called the Bridge House for a few pints of bitter. As he was standing at the bar leaning over to sip head off his pint he felt tap on the shoulder, "Ello Timmy, aw are ya?"

"You ar a bleedin sight for sore eyes. I heard you was out and I've been looking for ya. I ave a job that's right up your alley mate...interested?"

"I dunno if I'm interested Twiggy." His real name was Terry Wilkinson but everyone called him Twiggy, after the British model from the 60's and 70's. No matter how much beer or food he ingested he stayed extremely skinny.

"Me and Spanner, you'll remember Spanner from the old days, right Timmy?"

"Yeah, course I do," replied the big man.

"Well he's got his hands on a shooter (gun) and we're finking of aving a go at the payroll delivery at the Coop flour mill. It stops at the dock gate usually at about six o'clock in the morning on a payday. If we get to the gate watchman just before, tie him up, slap a little tape on his mouf; that way e should be quiet when they pull up. They roll the window down. You take the gun and shove it in the window and tell the driver to unlock the doors or you splash his brains all over the cab of the lorry. Me and Spanner will jump in, fill our duffle bags. Then all three of us jump in the parked motor car and we're away. What do ya fink Timmy?"

"Sounds slick Twig but I've,"...he wanted to say that he'd turned over a new leaf but he was afraid he'd lose his standing in the fraternity of local criminals. He'd be ostracized, or worse they'd laugh at him. He did not like to be made fun of.

"But what?" said the skinny crook to Timothy Green. "You can get a lot of porridge, for using a shooter in a robbery Twiggy and I'm not going back inside. Do you hear what I'm saying?" He started to get hot under the collar and his voice was getting uncharacteristically higher.

"Piss off Twiggy and leave me alone or I'll rip your bleedin head off your body. I'm not going back inside for you or anyone else." He left his full pint on the bar and walked straight out of the pub and on to a waiting bus back to his bedsit. Twiggy just stood there open mouthed and stunned. After a moment he realized that Timmy had left a full pint of beer so he took it and drank it and then walked out.

The next day was Saturday; Timothy went as usual to the reading and writing lesson at the convent. "Hello Timothy," she smiled at him and he just looked down at his shoes and walked behind her to the library.

"Is there something wrong?" she asked. "No," was the sharp reply.

"Yes there is Timothy, please tell me." "I'm good for nofink, only for fumping people and knocking eds together." He told Sister Nicola about the union job in the paint factory. "Isn't that a wonderful opportunity for you to double your income and have some responsibility?"

"No they want me cause all the blokes there are afraid of me. My job will be to intimidate them all into doing exactly what the union tells me and I tell them or they could wind up getting a fumping from ME!"

It's all I've ever been good for, fumping and thieving. Now I've met you and I know that if I do any of those fings you'd ave nothing to do w'iv me. I'm fed-up and feeling boxed in." He did not tell her about the offer of an armed robbery.

"I'm glad that I've had such a positive effect on you. Our friendship means a lot to me too."

"Are you always going to be a nun?"

"Timothy what do you mean?"

"Will you always be a nun?" "Of course. It's my calling, my life's work. Are you asking me if I'd ever give up my relationship with the Lord?"

"No I know you'd never do that, but will you always be a nun?"

"I've answered that question. Please let's read from this new book I found for you to read. It's a little harder than you have ever read before. Then we'll have you write a letter to a loved one or a friend that will help you understand how you can use all of the writing that you've learned over the past few months and yes it's become years hasn't it?" She was trying to change the subject. She was flustered and her face was turning beet red and she knew it. She excused herself for a while and stood in the washroom and looked in the mirror to see just how red her cheeks had become and then she sat down on the toilet seat and prayed silently, *"Lord what is happening here?"*

Chapter # 24 End of the line.

Several weeks later, Mary got a call at work from the principal at Jimmy's school. Could she come to the school and get Jimmy?

He'd been drinking and smoking at noon and had fallen asleep in class in the afternoon. She raced to the school, in a shocked daze. Everyone looked at her as she made her way down the hallways to the principal's office.

The receptionist greeted her by her first name; they knew each other from the bakery where Mary worked. "Hello Mary, Jimmy's in with Mr. Maitland." She just nodded and knocked on the door of the office. Mr. Maitland beckoned her to enter. Jimmy was sitting on a chair. His eyes were very red. He'd been crying and looked a little worse for wear. She didn't look at him, or he at her.

She spoke directly to the principal. "I'm sorry Mr. Maitland for my son's behavior; I wish I could say that this will not happen again but in perfect truth I'm not sure I can." The two never spoke, until they got in the car. She looked straight at him and said, "And you're smoking on top of everything else," and she burst into tears. He went to put his hand on her shoulder and she turned toward him and started to slap his head. She wouldn't stop, in anger, in fear, she kept on slapping. He put his hands up to protect himself but she just kept on until she was finally spent. She put her head on the steering wheel and cried. He just sat there stunned and confused. His lovely Mum was crazy. She had turned against him. He sat there looking out of the window and thought to himself, *"I'm leaving, quitting school and heading out on my own. I don't have to put up with this crap."*

They got home and Mary phoned Jack at the golf course, "Jack, it's Jimmy, he's drinking this time at school.

"Ow", said Jack. "Okay, I'll try to get home a little earlier tonight." Jimmy retreated to his bedroom. Jack got home and he and Mary stood in the kitchen. Jimmy could hear some of the conversation but not all of it. He knew that this was serious and he wished he could have heard more of it so that he could plan how he was going to get out of whatever punishment they had in store for him.

Jimmy came out of the bedroom for supper and sat at the kitchen table and tried to apologize. "Mum, I'm sorry I let you down again."

"Don't say you're sorry. You're only sorry you got caught. Jack and I want to speak with you after dinner." Nobody spoke all throughout the entire dinner, not a word. Jimmy opened the door to his room but Mary, interjected. "Jimmy come and sit down with us here in the living room." Jack sat down looking very awkward. He would have liked to crack a joke to lighten the mood but he thought better of it.

"Jimmy, Jack and I have decided to send you to live in England. I've phoned my aunt Maud and she and your uncle Frank have agreed to let you live with them." Mary started to cry again at the thought of letting her only child live in another country. Jimmy was relieved and quite excited at the thought of traveling back to London, England. This was not the punishment he'd anticipated at all. The only part he didn't like was that he had to earn the money for the airline ticket. Working at the golf course, fulltime, his school days were over!

Jack had him working in the back-shop cleaning golf clubs. Every time a member played golf he or she deposited their clubs back to the shop and they were cleaned before they were put away on the club racks. It was a job that was the lowest position at any golf course and way beneath a caddie which Jimmy considered himself to be. On the first day Jimmy poked his head into

Jack's GM office which was plush, full of odd clubs and golf merchandise samples of clothing that suppliers hoped Jack would bring into the Pro shop and sell. Jimmy loved the way that it looked and felt; like Jack it was colourful and classy.

"Jack, does anyone need a caddie, a genius putting caddie?"

"Oh, no Jimmy you'll be staying in the back shop until you earn enough to get a ticket to London."

"No caddying for you. I can't trust out on the course where I can't see you."

"Oh Jack, c'mon, you know I can make good tips for being on the course with the players."

"Exactly that's why you're not allowed, just in case you buy booze with it. The only work available to you here at the course is in the back shop." Jack picked up the phone indicating to the boy that the conversation was over. Jimmy disappeared into the back shop to the never-ending golf clubs to wash and put away. Later that day Jimmy tried again, "Can I still play golf after my hours?"

"Yes, but if I catch you playing for money, I'll fire your sorry, skinny ass out of here, got it?"

"Yes."

"You'll have to find a job in town, pumping gas or filling grocery bags to make that money you need to get that airline ticket back to England." Jimmy again retreated to the back shop and that sea of clubs to wash.

Weeks went by and while Jimmy wanted desperately to join his friends the Kirbys and other ne'er do wells for a few beers and some of that White Lightening that old man Kirby gave them, he tried very hard to keep his nose clean. He was excited at the thought of going back to England; he had a romantic memory of the place. The young boy was in for a shock. Finally, after some weeks working in the back shop he had enough for a ticket to London's Heathrow airport. He worked for a few weeks more for some spending money.

The big day came and Mary and Jack both took the day off to drive him to New Orleans to catch his flight to England. He'd never been on Lake Pontchartrain Causeway, which was a thirty-five-mile bridge over Lake Pontchartrain. That project was the pride of the state of Louisiana and it was finally complete on January 20, 1955. The bridge seemed to go on forever. Jack had the top down on his convertible, since it was a warm Louisiana spring day. Jack was dressed from head to toe in purple, purple golf shirt underneath a purple sweater, purple slacks and white shoes with a purple saddle on the shoes. Jimmy smiled to himself and thought *as hard as I tried I could never be that bold in my dress but it somehow suited Jack.* Jimmy loved him all the more for it. He wanted so much to be like Jack but he wasn't his father. They all just pretended he was. Mary had on a light summer dress, and her long hair hung down to the middle of her back. Some of his friends told him his mum was hot. It made him sick to his stomach that anyone would think of her in those terms. She cried for a lot of the hour drive over the causeway. When they arrived, Jack parked the car and Mary and Jimmy went inside the airport.

"Be good for your Auntie Maud and Uncle Frank son please."

"I will, I promise." He was carrying his old Titleist golf clubs and a medium size suitcase.

"I'm truly sorry it's come to this but I really believe this is the best thing for you Jimmy. Make the most of it."

"I will Mum, I will." He was not really paying attention to her. He was trying to look at the departure time and where he needed to be. She kept hugging him and crying a little. Finally, Jack showed up and cracked a funny joke about finally getting rid of his aching back, and pointed at Jimmy and did his funny little jig. Mary rolled her eyes and Jimmy pushed against Jack and their eyes met and they both realized that this was actually happening and both had to look away. They all stood for a moment not knowing what to say.

Jack said, "Jimmy, life is like putting. It's straight back and straight through to the hole. Always play it straight and you can't go too far wrong." The tension was getting palpable. Jimmy needed to move to the gate.

He hugged Jack and then his mother for a long time; he knew he couldn't dare look at her. He turned on his heels and said, "Love you guys. See you soon," and left for his gate to the airplane. He never looked back, he couldn't.

Mary fell into Jack and cried, "What have we done?"

"The right thing Mary, you needed to get him away from the influence he was all wrapped up in here." With his arm around her they walked back to the carpark and the thirty-five-mile ride across Lake Pontchartrain Causeway. Not a word was spoken until she eventually cried and broke the silence with a question.

"What will happen to him?"

Jack said, "You know he's not your little boy any more. I've seen him grow and blossom into a sneaky little rascal that has the where-with-all to make his way in the world, whether in London, England or in Covington, Louisiana. That is of course as long as he keeps off the booze."

Mary looked long and hard at Jack and she said, "I hope you are right. I've spoken with Maud and Frank and they are poor as church mice. They said he'll have to pay rent and work plus they want him to go to night school and pay for it himself."

"He won't have any spare cash to buy drink," said Jack with a smirk. Then he paused and followed up with, "That boy is in for one hell of a shock."

Chapter #25 'Eaven elp us

Sister Nicola made her way back to the library and found the big man sitting in the same spot trying to read the book she brought to the lesson. "You were a long time, I fought you'd left."

"Oh I just had a couple of things to deal with before we carried on Timothy, sorry about that. Okay let's begin reading. Start with the preface and read it out loud to me. Let me look over your shoulder." She positioned herself so that she could see the page. He could smell her, it was a simple clean soap smell, but combined with her own natural body smell, he found it intoxicating. She followed his slow and deliberate reading cadence, using his finger to keep his place. Occasionally she'd interject a positive word of encouragement. "Good," if he'd stumble or had difficulty with a word, "That's it you've got it," she'd say and smile at him.

This tiresome lesson went on for over thirty minutes until mercifully, "Oye ain't it time for a nice cuppa?"

"Yes of course," she replied and ran out into the communal kitchen of the convent to put the kettle on and look for any spare biscuits or cake. Within a few minutes she hurried back with a small tray holding a large brown tea pot covered by a hand-knitted tea cozy, milk in a small jug with a broken handle and a glass sugar bowl with two teaspoons sticking out of the sugar. There in the middle of the tray was a small plate with several broken biscuits on it, one shortbread biscuit and several digestives, her favourite.

"Fanks," was his only unthinking reply to the tea and treats.

"Let's move on to the writing for the last part of the lesson, okay Timothy?"

"Yeah all right," was his uninterested flat reply.

"Let's pretend that you're going to write to a friend or a loved one inviting them to your party, okay?"

Der..."No you've misspelled dear, you forgot the 'a'."

"Oh alright. Dear Sister Nicola." He read the words as he wrote them. "No, Timothy I wanted you to write to a loved one or a friend."

"You're my only true friend," he responded. That melted her heart and she spoke no more as he went on. "*I wonder if you are always going to be a nun because if you are then I will always want to be your friend because of your duty to the God you serve. If you decide to stop being a nun, I want to marry you and look after you for the rest of my life. After I am dead then you can go back to God and be a nun again. W'iv love and respect T. Green.*"

All the sentences ran together, no grammar or punctuation just words and some spelled wrong. She stood there looking at the words on the page, and didn't move. She even forgot to take a breath, just for a moment. Tears ran down her cheeks and onto the page. She quickly turned away and left the room. Timothy waited for the rest of the lesson time but she didn't come back. So, he ate all of the biscuits left on the plate and then walked back to his bedsit in a cold drizzle downpour and he didn't even notice the rain. The week went by and he went to work every day filling barrels of paint, mostly battleship grey for the Royal Navy. He also did his union business and kept the motley crew on the paint fillers floor in line.

Saturday came around and the big man lumbered to the convent for what he hoped would be an hour of bliss with his little penguin. He knocked on the old oak door. Mother Superior opened it and asked Timothy to step in out of the wind and rain.

"I'm ere for me lesson."

"I'm so sorry Timothy she isn't here."

"Where is she?"

"She has gone home to her family."

"Where's at?"

"I'm sorry my dear I can't divulge that kind of personal information."

"Is she coming back?"

"I think we are going to have to see; only time will tell." Timothy looked shocked and dejected. His head went down on his big chest and he slowly got up and said,

"Okay, fanks Mo'ver." As he walked to the front door of the convent he thought to himself, *I've done it naw, I've frightened her away.*

As he walked the damp grey streets back to his dreary bedsit he felt a salty sensation on the corner of his lips. After a moment he realized for the first time in his adult life he was crying. He missed her and loved her. He thought of her soft white face and her clear green eyes, her small white hands, and her smell, he loved her smell. The thought of never seeing her again was too much for him. He heard a sound coming from somewhere inside that was too painful to acknowledge. He just gulped for a huge breath of air that would stop the emotion of loss from overwhelming him. He wasn't able to stop the tears; the sleeves of his worn coat just brushed them away as he walked.

A week went by and he wasn't able to keep the thought of her out of his head, *I fink I'd better keep reading and practicing me writing just in case she comes back.* He thought to himself.

He remembered her last name and she spoke about her family coming from East Sussex. He seemed to remember her mentioning going to school in the small city of Crowborough. He reasoned that he should take the train to Crowborough and see if he could find her and tell he was sorry that he had spoken out of turn. If she'd come back, he'd never mention anyfink about marrying or stopping being a nun. They could go back to the way it was.

The following Saturday, was a warm summer day. He put on his worn second-hand suit that the Screws had given him when they released him from Wormwood Scrubs prison. His shirt was wrinkled but he thought, *"If I keep my Jacket buttoned up no one will see it."* He set off very early on the bus to the Westham underground station. The tube took him directly to Victoria Street Station on the Jubilee line and then he took a train to the small town of Crowborough. He got off the train and found a café that served a good full English breakfast; he drank a couple of cups of tea and leaned back for a smoke. He asked the bloke behind the counter, who was the cook and small café owner, if he knew the Scrivens family.

"Naw, never eard of them mate. Do you want any more tea, and if not, can I collect for the breakfast?"

"Yeah course you can, aw much is it?"

"Two and seven"

"Two schillings and seven pence just for a couple of eggs and a few rashers of bacon, you're taking the piss ain't yaw?"

"Ear the prices are up on the board. You should ave looked at the prices before you ordered if you fink it's too much money." Timothy threw a half a crown (2 schillings and six pence) on the counter.

"You're a penny short," said the café owner.

"Bollocks!" said the big man in a threatening manner as he walked out the door and took three steps and then in his head popped Sister Nicola. *"What would she say? She'd be very disappointed in me."* He stopped, turned around and went back in the café and handed the owner a three-pence bit (3 penny coin) and walked out onto the street.

He lit a cigarette and inhaled deeply. It helped him think. *"I'll go to the town hall; aw it's closed it's bleedin Saturday ain't it?* Then he looked down the street and he saw the police station. He thought, *"I can't go in there, somefink bad will appen."*

He'd come this far and so he plucked up his courage and went to a place he never thought he'd ever visit willingly. "Ello Gov'ner I'm looking for an old mate of mine, Mr. Scrivens. Do you know where he lives?"

"No but if I did I wouldn't tell you. If Mr. Scrivens is a mate of yours he'd tell you where he lives wouldn't he?"

The big man smiled and said, "Yeah I supposed he would."

"Now young man," said the old gray-haired sergeant, "why are you looking for Mr. Scrivens?"

He was caught, and so he thought *I'll tell em the truth.* "Ok, Plod," he said in a mocking manner. "Nicola Scrivens is a nun from the Ursuline Convent and believe it or not she is a very good friend of mine. She came home to Crowborough for a term and I've missed her and I wanted to get in touch with her and see if she is alright. That is the truth." The sergeant looked at him for a while and said,

"What if she doesn't want to get in touch with you my lad?"

"Well hopefully she'll tell me that when I knock on her bleedin door won't she?" and he turned and walked out of the police station knowing they would not help him at all.

Then it dawned on him she is a nun, *"I'll go to the Catholic Church and ask them."* After a long walk he finally found the local Catholic church. He entered the building and saw the priest at the front doing some adjustments on the altar getting ready for the Saturday evening Mass.

"Er, ello my name is Timothy Green and I'm looking for Sister Nicola, Nicola Scrivens, do you know where she lives?"

"Yes, she lives in the Ursuline Convent in London."

"Well yeah normally she does but she's come ome for a time. Can you please tell me where she lives?"

"No, my son I cannot. What I will do is tell them you are looking for them. What is your name?"

"But I'm only ere for the day." The big man was angry. He was that close, "*That old bloke knows where she is,*" he thought to himself, "*and he won't tell me. This is ridiculous; I'm going for a beer, maybe several.*"

He found his way to the pub called the White Hart Inn. It was noisy and busy for a Saturday early afternoon on market day. He pushed through to the bar and ordered a pint of Brown Ale. He took a deep drink and then lit a cigarette. He leaned comfortably on the bar and several people got out of his way and made room for him.

"Anything else?" asked the barman. "No, not unless you know where I can find a bloke called Scrivens." The barman was caught off guard and just stood there with his mouth open.

"He's standing beside you."

"Hello I'm Sir Charles Scrivens, why would you be looking for me?"

"Oh Blimey, um, I'm a friend of Nicola's, Sister Nicola that is. I wanted to ave a word w'iv er, if you could see your way clear to letting er know. I've come down on the train today, and I wanted to see if she's doing alright, since she left London in an hurry." He realized he was talking too much and shut up.

Sir Charles stood back and looked at him and said, "How do you know my daughter?"

"Well, she as been teaching me to read and write. To tell the truf, she as been teaching me for the past few years.

She's done so much for me I wanted to make sure she was alright, Gov'ner, er I mean Sir Charles."

"Finish your ale my good man and let's see if my daughter Sister Nicola wants to see you."

Chapter #26. The way you remember.

Jimmy was sitting in the window seat on the Pan Am flight to London's Heathrow airport via Amsterdam.

As the food service began the pretty stewardess placed his tray on the pull-out table and asked him "What would you like to drink?"

"What are my options?" he replied craftily.

"We have tea, coffee, soft drink or beer?"

He thought he'd take a chance and quickly said, "Beer," watching her reaction because of his age. The next thing he knew she placed a can of Heineken beer on his tray and he stared at it in disbelief.

After he'd eaten his dinner she came back and said, "Can I get you anything else?"

"Another beer?" he asked curiously expecting her or someone to say, "*Hey how old you are anyway?*" She didn't. She just brought him another Heineken. He fell asleep for most of the trip to Amsterdam. He got off the flight feeling sleepy and a little lost. He checked for the last leg of the flight to Heathrow, and then he spotted a sandwich bar. He stood in line and took a tray and reached in for a turkey sandwich and then spotted the drinks in the next compartment including beer. He tried to look cool and grown up as he reached for yet another beer. He paid the cashier and found a seat and ate his turkey sandwich and slowly drank his beer at 9:30 in the morning. *He thought to himself, I really like being treated like an adult.* It wouldn't be long before he wished he wasn't treated so grown up.

He made his flight to Heathrow and was greeted by his Aunt Maud and Uncle Frank. From all the stories told to him over the years he felt deeply connected to these people but they didn't know him at all. They were wary in light of his mother's colourful description of a possible drinking problem and his boozy breathe which was noticed when Maud hugged him on his arrival. Frank drove the borrowed car from a friend since he was unable to afford one of his own. He was a very nervous driver and he was unsure of every turn and lane change. He constantly asked his wife. She obviously didn't know how to drive or the rules of the road either but tried to be positive until half way on the forty-five-minute drive. She got frustrated with him and told him to figure it out himself. He never asked again.

They arrived and at 57 Eltham Palace Road, in south London.

Jimmy asked, "Aren't we going to 173 Herbert Road in Plumstead?"

Maud laughed, "Jimmy we haven't lived there since my mum and dad passed away some time ago. They lived in a two up two down maisonette, government housing or council housing as they referred to it."

He carried his small suitcase and his old golf clubs toward the house and Frank said to him, "What do you intend to do with those things?"

"Play golf." "You must be joking, working class people like us don't play golf," and he laughed at the thought. It reminded Jimmy all those years ago when he stepped off the plane in San Antonio and Jed's hired hand made fun of the way he was dressed, he felt embarrassed.

They climbed the steep staircase to the top of the flat and his Aunt Maud told him that his Aunt Dora lived downstairs with his Uncle Dick. He remembered him well, the uncle that wanted to be called Richard but everyone called him Dick. She went on to say that Aunt Lily and Uncle Sid lived around the corner next to Aunt Chris and Uncle Phil. Uncle Phil was new. Aunt Chris had been divorced and had remarried. Finally, Aunt Eva and your Uncle Jock live just down the road. Jimmy thought to himself, "*Well mum certainly had that part of the story right. They are all together.*"

"Put your things in the bedroom for now." He walked into a small room with metal bunk-beds pushed against the wall and a small wardrobe in the corner. There was a bedside table with a lamp on it and a picture of a brown and white pointer dog in a golden frame hanging from a string attached to the picture rail. There was flowered wallpaper that made the room look even darker than it should have with its small window onto the street.

She stood behind him as he set his small suitcase on the bed and said, "Am I sharing with someone?"

"Of course, you are sharing with our son, your cousin John."

"Oh," said Jimmy, trying to sound not too disappointed at the limited accommodation.

"Jimmy, Uncle Frank and I are not wealthy people. This flat is all we have and it only has two bedrooms."
"Yes, yes of course I'm grateful that you've taken me in."
She could see that he thought he deserved more.

A week went by and he visited several golf courses looking for work as a caddie or even heaven forbid back shop work. He was stunned to find out that almost all of the golf courses in his area were not golf courses like in the U.S. at all. In the states most, if not all, were businesses owned by a company or by people who ran them for profit with a mindset of service to golfers. In England they were clubs owned by the members which were run by boards without much consideration for profit but rather to provide a place for members to golf at the lowest possible cost to each member. In the U.S., members would pay thousands every year to be a member. In England it was more like hundreds. The bottom line was that none of them were looking for caddies and they didn't have back shops or back shop employees, since everyone took their golf clubs home with them. Jimmy just shook his head and became more and more disenchanted with the prospect for a golf career in England.

Another week went by and Maud asked "Jimmy what are your plans?"

"I think I better get back to school."

"Oh, I'm sorry son but you're too old for school here in England. You'll have to get a job, a full-time job. I'll need some rent money, and money to cover your food. You are another mouth to feed. You can't expect Uncle Frank and I to pay for that." He was speechless and stunned. He scoured the papers for any job opportunities and went out for a few job interviews but he was woefully under qualified for any job that he wanted. He felt the pressure of paying for his room and board. He thought he'd be treated as family and they'd simply take care of him but no, he had to pay his own way. He thought them uncaring; little did he realize this was the plan from the start. A little tough love and a reality check, all organized by his mother.

One evening Uncle Jock came by and he heard him speaking with his Aunt Maud in the kitchen. "Yes please speak with him in the front room." Jock came into the room. Jimmy was sitting by the only source of heat in the entire flat a small gas fireplace.

"Jimmy I got a job for you in the Royal Victoria Dock at the Coop Floor Mill."

"Doing what?" "As a cleaner. It's decent money." "You want me to be a cleaner?"

"Yes," said his aunt, "any job that you can get wages for is a plus. You cannot afford to be picky Jimmy. It's been three weeks since you arrived."

"When do I start?"

"Monday at seven o'clock in the morning. You have to catch two buses to Woolwich and then take the foot tunnel to the other side and it's a short walk to the dock gate. I'll go with you for your first week."

Jimmy just said, "Okay thanks."

Uncle Frank woke him for his first day of work and he had to call him four times. He still didn't like getting out of his warm bed. Finally, he got up and Frank told him that his Uncle Jock was waiting for him at the bottom of the stairs. He had no time for tea or toast or even a wash. Off he ran following behind his Uncle Jock for his first day of real work. As he sat on the bus, he was emptied of optimism. *This can't be happening to me, I was going to be a golf pro. People looked to me for putting lessons. I worked at a high-end golf course and lived in a nice ranch style home on a quiet tree-lined street. Jack Parker is my step-father and he's the real deal in Covington. I'm in London docklands and certainly not in Covington, Louisiana.*

Upon arrival he was issued two pair of brown cleaner's overalls, an industrial dust pan and broom and a cloth bag of duster rags. A man, who in Jimmy's opinion wasn't able to spell golf, led him to the second floor and a row of huge machines. Jimmy's job was to continually dust the machines and sweep the floor of the dust that was continually seeping from these machines. The dust started with wheat from the ships that made the trip from North America to the London dockland and after it had been passed through the myriad of machines came out as soft, white flour. It ended up in eighty-pound sacks that made the product for the Coop Floor Mill. Jimmy stood there and wanted to cry. What had he done! The day didn't get better. The nose-drubbing got worse.

When he stood for a moment leaning on the broom, the foreman walked by and shouted at him, "Oye you with the broom get busy or else." He was afraid of the 'or else' and it made him feel even more down about his situation. Days dragged into weeks, weeks into months. Jimmy kept trying to find work at a golf course but to no avail. He paid for his room and board but there was very little money left over. There was never enough to allow him to succumb to his tendency for over consumption of alcohol. His financial circumstances caused him to be a moderate drinker, much to his aunt and mother's delight. Jimmy was reverting back to the beige teenager he had been before golf. He was sinking back into blandness and he was losing his confidence and the more time that passed the more confidence he was losing. He felt desperate and decided it was time to get back to Louisiana and his life of golf. This life of cleaning and sweeping and living with these poor people was not going to be his lot in life.

He got home to find his Aunt Maud cooking supper for him, his cousin and his Uncle Frank.

After supper, he made a pronouncement, "I've decided to go back to the U.S." He said it awkwardly; he blurted it out, which made it sound more like a threat than surrender to his circumstance.

She stood up in front of him and folded her arms and said, "Yes, you most certainly can return but you have to save for the cost of your flight all the while paying me for your room and board." Jimmy felt he was being railroaded, which he was. His aunt didn't want the money but she was fighting hard to keep him from going back into that lifestyle that his mother was so afraid would be the end of him. Maud did it for her Mary in the U.S.

Jimmy realised what she was saying, "But Aunt Maud it will take me months to save that kind of money." She smiled to herself and as straight-faced as she could muster said, "Well, son it depends how badly you want to get home now, doesn't it?" He felt he'd been kicked in the solar plexes, all the air left his body and he wanted to cry, but instead got up and slowly went into his small dark bedroom. He crawled into bed, pulled the covers over his head and sobbed from the wretched sadness of missing his mum and Jack and feeling like he had lost his identity and dignity by making this move to England. The next morning, he awoke early with a steely determination to do whatever he needed to do to get home. He took the same two buses to the Woolwich foot tunnel and walked under the Thames along with thousands of other factory workers. Then he walked toward the dock gate that housed the Coop Flour Mill. It was early and still dark as he approached the dock gate as usual. As he walked up toward the gate from Silvertown Way, the main road, he felt darkness close in above and around him. Something menacing grabbed him almost knocking him down, whatever the thing was that had a hold of him, dragged him back toward the main road and then across the road to a waiting dark van. He was trying to wriggle out of the grasp. One arm got completely free of the overcoat he was wearing but the something grabbed the free arm and based on the way he was gripped he knew it was useless to struggle. It threw him roughly into the back of the van and the door smashed behind him violently. There were two men in the front of the van; he didn't recognise either of them. They seemed almost as shocked as Jimmy was. The passenger door opened and in jumped a very large man that Jimmy recognised immediately. Jimmy lost his breath. He shook as he had been confronted by a specter of irrational fear. He was having trouble processing what had just happened, and he couldn't make sense of this at all. He just sat in the back of the van and stared at his worst nightmare which happened to be sitting in the same van.

"Drive," said Timothy Green in a flat monotone manner, "Drive to my bedsit." The van raced away. At some point the van stopped and out got the big man. The back door opened and he reached in and grabbed the skinny teenager. He roughly hauled him up the two flights of stairs to his small dingy bedsit room. It contained a bed, a small chest of drawers and a large wardrobe. It also had a small industrial type sink in the room and a dirty hand towel hanging on a hook above the sink.

"Sit down!"

"I'm not staying long. I'll stand," said Jimmy with as much bravery as he could pretend to have.

"I'll tell you aw long you're staying for lad, got it?"

"Yes," said Jimmy.

"My aunt and uncle will be looking for me."

"They will find you but only after I've got what I want. Where is she?"

"Where is who?" Jimmy realized immediately that was the wrong thing to say and he winced and thought it might produce a thump.

"You know who I mean. Where is your mo'ver?"

"She lives in the United States of America," he said like it should intimidate his abductor.

"Where in the United States of America?" said the big man in a mocking tone."

"My step-dad and my mum have moved and I don't know where they moved to."

"You lying little git. Tell me where they live. I've got to speak to her; I'm not going to let you go until you give me an address where I can contact her."

"You're kidnapping me?"

"Call it what you like, me old son, but you ain't going anywhere until you tell me where she is." He was afraid; he didn't know exactly why but he had an irrational fear of this fellow that was from somewhere deep inside of him.

The big man lunged toward him, his eyes bulging, "Tell me!"

"Covington, Louisiana".

"Address, tell me the address." "1410 Nolan Road," Jimmy spilled the beans. He had to as the fear was overwhelming, and he would do anything to get away from this monster of a man.

"C'mon, I'll take you back to the Victoria Dock; you can get back to work."

It never dawned on Timothy that this may be perceived as kidnapping, until the boy mentioned the word 'kidnapping'. It put the wind up him, although he tried not to show it to the boy. He most definitely did not want to go back to Wormwood Scrubs or any other prison.

"What are you are going to do with my mother?" asked Jimmy on the bus ride back down Silvertown way to the Coop Flour mill.

"You sound like a bleedin American," said the Big Man.

"I need to get this mess sorted out wiv your mo'ver once and for all."

"You better not hurt her." Timothy Green's eyes flashed and he wanted to lash out at the lad but in this public place he knew he couldn't.

"She was the one that ran away from me, remember," he said quietly as he leaned into the boy.

"How did you know I'd be at the dock gate this morning?"

"I didn't, I was looking at a job and I saw you."

"What job?" asked a naïve Jimmy. "Never mind, you get back to work and you tell your mo'ver I'll be getting in touch." The big man pulled the cord on the double decker bus indicating he wanted off at the next stop and Jimmy carried on to the Victoria dock stop and went to work, albeit two hours late.

Jimmy couldn't wait to get home to tell his Aunt Maud this story.

"Did he hurt you?" she asked.

"Well, not really although when he dragged me to the van and threw me inside it was a little rough." He could see his aunt was very afraid. Her eyes got big and her lip trembled.

"I should phone mum. I know it's very expensive but I think I should phone her."

"Yes the cost isn't a consideration," said his aunt.

The phone rang almost twenty times and he realized that she wasn't at home. He hung up.

"Can I call Jack at work?"

"Yes okay but please make it short."

"Ok, I will."

"Hello Jack."

"Yes this is Jack Parker."

"Jack it's Jimmy. Please tell mum that I was approached by Timothy Green today while I was going to work. He forced me to tell him where you guys lived. I'm sorry Jack I was so afraid."

"It's okay buddy, I understand."

"I can't talk long Jack but I really miss you and mum." "We missed you too flat-belly." That made Jimmy smile. With that Jack hung up the phone, Jimmy stood there for a while holding the phone not wanting the call to end.

Jack wondered how he was going to tell her.

Chapter #27 Reality

Sir Charles drove the big man to a country estate about seven miles outside of Crowborough. As he drove through two huge brick pillars, there before him was a neat ribbon of crushed clean stones and the road that led to the estate. Timothy Green had never seen such a huge house, never mind one with such elegance. He counted twelve sets of enormous windows across the front of the stately house. Sir Charles drove up past the house toward a low building with five garage doors. A man in a butler's uniform ran out to greet Sir Charles and held the door to the Rover 3.5 open while he got out. He looked over at Timothy and said, "Please wait here with my man," pointing at the man in the butler's outfit.

In a very highbrow accent the hired man said, "If sir could please wait here while I park the car in the garage." Timothy smiled it wasn't often that he was called sir.

Timothy was intimidated being at the elegant estate. When the hired man returned Timothy simply said to him,

"Nice gaff."

The butler just grunted, and said, "Yes it's a lovely stately house." He looked down his very long pointed nose at this man that was obviously below his education and station in life.

Timothy heard a door open. He quickly turned around and there was a young beautiful lady. It was her.

"I've never seen your 'air before." Her hair was a dark brown and was cut just above her neckline. She was wearing a summer weight frock and she looked stunning.

"Timothy why are you here? How did you find me?"

"I ave me ways."

"Please come and walk with me." She led Timothy to the rear of the huge house to the beautiful traditional English gardens.

"How have you been Timothy?"

"I've been lovely, yeah, lovely. I fink I frightened you away from the convent wiv my letter writin." As she looked back she could see that her father was keeping his eye on her in the gardens.

"Yes your marriage proposal was a little bit shocking. I must say it was lovely but shocking."

"I know. Why would a beautiful, fine lady like you ave anyfink to do with a big lug like me?"

"It's not that Timothy. You're married and I'm a nun. Doesn't it seem unlikely that we could be a couple? I've grown to love you but not in the way that you want me too. You are a married man. I understand that she ran off and left you but it doesn't negate the fact that you are married."

"What does ne-gate mean?"

"Oh Timothy it just means that the fact is that you are a married man and nothing can change that. Even if I wasn't a committed Christian and in the Ursuline Order you'd still be a married man. There is no future for us no matter and that's why I left. I was confused by my feelings. I needed a break."

"I didn't realise that you come from such a posh family."

"Yes, my father, you met him, is Sir Charles Scrivens and this is our family estate."

"Your far'ver is keeping his on eye me isn't he?" He laughed nervously.

"Yes I'm afraid he is," she smiled at him and it melted him again.

"Well ere's why I'm really ere. I just want fings to go back to the way they was, that's all. I shouldn't have declared my feelings and I know I've frightened you away. You've shown me kindness I've never seen before; you've never let me down or left me wiv-out your elp. You've kept me away from crime and my old lifestyle and I've no intention of going back. But to face the rest of my life wivout seeing you is," he paused not knowing what words to say, "is, is too hard!"

She looked at him and said, "This is too difficult. Please leave, please."

She ran to the house and disappeared for a moment. Sir Charles came out and said, "My man Brooks will drive you into town or to the train station whatever suits you. Thank you for coming." And he turned his back on the big man and went inside the monstrous house. As Timothy sat on the luxurious leather seat in the old Rover automobile all he felt was sadness and confusion at this turn of events.

"Where would sir like to be dropped off?"

"At the train station...fanks!"

He took the train back to Victoria Street station and then the tube to Westham but Timothy missed the last bus from Westham back to his bedsit and had to walk the thirty minutes. During the walk he made a decision. He'd go back to his life of criminality. Without her in his life going straight had no benefit to him. As he started to think about what he'd do he remembered a conversation in a pub with Twiggy and a possible job at the Co-op flour mill and a gun. He decided that he needed to find Twiggy.

******

Three days later he found Twiggy in the Kings Arms in Bethnal Green High Street.

"Twiggy I've decided to take on that job w'iv you and Spanner. Let's case the place this week and get the lay of the land. Once we know where to park the car, where the payroll lorry pulls up, how many guards in the gatehouse, I can take care of the rough stuff. I'll handle the gun and the threatening. You and Spanner get inside and get the payroll. We'll split the grab three ways and be done with it."

"Oye Timmy I fought you was done with the rob. Last time I saw you didn't want anyfink to do with it."

"Twig, I was being stupid and a bit of a dreamer. I've come to my senses."

"Okay good," said Twiggy, "Game on. Pick me up on Tuesday morning, early. We'll wait for the payroll lorry to check in w'iv the dock gate, see how long it takes, where we'll position ourselves to get the job done and to get away."

"I'm on the afternoon shift at the paint factory." "You won't afta go to work after we pull this one off Timmy, me old mate."

Timothy Green looked at his chum with disdain and said, "Packing in my job would be a tipoff to the old bill. I'll stay at work for a month or two's gone by. Then I'll be off enjoying my share of the loot."

"Right," said Twiggy as he downed the last of his Brown Ale and left the King Arms pub, got into his old beat up Ford Transit van and drove off. Tuesday morning came and Timothy made himself a strong cup of tea with sterilized milk and lots of sugar. All he had left in his cupboard was a dry third of a Hovis loaf of bread and a small piece of hard cheese. He ate the food and then poured himself another cup and had just sat down when he heard a vehicle pull up outside the bedsit. The motor was loud and he realised that Twiggy's van was in desperate need of a new muffler. He looked out the window to make sure it was him and then he left his tea to get cold, grabbed his coat and made his way downstairs to the loudly running van.

"Ello Twig, bleedin cold this morning ain't it? Where is Spanner?"

"We have to pick him up on the way." All three of the thugs arrived thirty minutes before the weekly payroll van made its delivery to the hundreds of men waiting for their weekly pay packets full of cash. Twiggy turned off the headlights and the motor and they waited. The three men were sitting in the vehicle complaining about the weather when suddenly the big man flew out of the van and ran across the road dodging transport lorries and grabbed a young factory worker by the coat and dragged him back to the van. His two colleagues were flabbergasted especially when he barked at them to drive to his bedsit with the young man sitting wide-eyed and stunned in the back of the dirty old Ford van. Twiggy and Spanner just stared in disbelief at each other, but they knew better than to utter a word. They pulled up outside the bedsit. Green got out hurriedly, ran to the back of the van and grabbed the young fellow.

Spanner shouted, "What the bleedin ell are you doing, Timmy?"

"I'll meet up w'iv you both tonight at the pub," as he dragged the young man up the stairs to his bedsit. The van drove away and the two crooks just looked at each other and Twiggy said, "What was that all about?"

"I dunno," answered the one they called Spanner.

*****

The door opened to the Kings Arms pub and in walked Timothy Green. As he entered he saw the two men he was looking for standing by the one-armed bandit putting two shilling pieces into the machine and hoping for a win. "Oye you two, you're wasting your hard-earned money ain't ya?"

"Hello Timmy," says Twiggy, "What was all that business today w'iv the lad from the dock gate?"

"Never mind that. I'm ere to let you know I'm out of the Co-op heist. You two are on your own." "Timmy what are you talking about. You're changing your mind more than my dad changes his string vest. Blimey, you're in, you're out, make your mind up once and for all."

"I ave and I'm out and I won't be changing it again. You're on your own." Timothy Green left without even ordering a beer.

Chapter #28 .44 Magnum

Mary came home from the bakery café tired and dead on her feet. She dropped her hand bag and the bag of groceries on the floor of the kitchen and just sat on the lazy boy recliner and said to herself, "*I just need a five-minute rest before I get the dinner ready.*" She heard a noise coming from the bedroom and she tensed every muscle in her body. She froze. The door opened and out came Jack. "You scared the living daylights out of me. What on earth are you doing home that this hour?"

"I have to speak with you Mary." She instantly defaulted to her old fear that Jack was leaving her for another. "I got a call from Jimmy today. He was confronted by...," he hesitated knowing that she would go into a fearful tailspin.

"By, whom?"

"He was confronted by your husband in England, Timothy Green."

"Oh no, is he alright?"

"Mary, he told him where we live. He gave him this address." She wasn't able to process what he said or the implications of those words for a moment or two and then it hit her.

"He knows where we live. Why would Jimmy tell him?"

"He told him because he was afraid for his life." Then she realized that her only son was in danger and now so were they. She stood and then all the air left her body.

She sat down again, put her head in her hands and rocked back and forth. "We need to leave; we need to get going right now!"

"No, Mary, we aren't going anywhere. This is America; we have the right to protect ourselves."

"How can we protect ourselves?" "With a gun. I bought one this afternoon and put in my top drawer of the bedroom dresser. It's loaded and ready to go. It has a safety lock on it and I'll show you how to unlock the safety and use it."

"A gun, you want me to fire a gun? No, I can't. I'm afraid of guns."

Jack looked at her sympathetically and said, "You'll have to decide what you are most afraid of, him or a gun."

She just sat there rocking back and forth. "I need to get Jimmy away from him." Jack tried to reassure her.

"He didn't hurt him, so I think he's okay."

"Jack what are we going to do? I can't live like this."

"We are going to live our lives and protect ourselves as best we can. I'm going to talk to the Sheriff Vance, since he's a member of the club and owes me a few favours. Now please let me show you the gun and how this safety works."

After a few minutes and with lots of explanation that she couldn't possibly hurt herself or Jack by firing the 44 Magnum accidently, she held it and nearly dropped it from the weight of the gun.

She looked at Jack and said, "Fire it, I can't even hold the bloody thing it's so heavy."

"You'll get used to it; we'll go to a gun range."

The first time at the gun range no matter how much Jack encouraged her to fire the gun, she couldn't. Fear stopped her. On the second visit it happened. She actually pulled the trigger. The gun exploded. She knew it was going to be loud but the jolt that she received from the magnum was like an electrical shock. It rocked her body. The gun started to fly back over her shoulder.

Jack yelled at her, "Mary hold it tighter!"

She fired it again, and then a third time. "Did I hit the target?"

Jack laughed and put his arm around her and said, "Not even close!"

On the ride home Jack began to comfort her with a plan, "Okay Mary, the gun will always be in the top drawer of my dresser, in with my socks, with the safety on. If anytime I'm not home and you feel threatened get the gun."

Mary silently hoped that a need for the gun would never arise, but somewhere deep inside she knew he would come. "Jack, I am so afraid of him but I still don't think I could use the gun if he did show up."

"Mary, you'll do what you'll need to do if and when the occasion arises. Let's hope it doesn't."

Weeks went by and no news came. Mary phoned Maud and chatted with her and Jimmy, even though it was very expensive.

Mary got home and on the kitchen counter was a pile of letters, mostly bills and final overdue notices. Jack wasn't a prompt payer of their outstanding bills. Mary mindlessly went through the small stack and noticed a letter from a child or least that is what she thought. She picked up the letter, and it was addressed simply to Mary at her home address in Covington. As she was opening the letter she realized who it was from. All these years later he was still after her. A shudder ran through her body, and her stomach turned and she felt like she needed a toilet sooner than later.

> Mary
>
> I saw your boy, I recognised him right away, on his way to work. He told me where you are. I've done me time at the scrubs and I ain't going back ever. I know you are with another bloke. You left England and me for a new life and it's time we got a few things straightened out. Im coming to Amerika. I know where you are.
> Tim

She stood still but her insides were cramping, her head was spinning, and she wanted to run again but Jack wouldn't hear of it.

Chapter #29 The comeuppance.

The big man went every week on Saturday to the Ursuline Convent. He knocked and he'd be greeted with a warm smile and a "Hello Timothy, I'm afraid she has not returned as of yet." This went on for several weeks.

Then one day, Sister Nicola opened the door and he quickly said, "Hello Sister. I'm only ere for me lesson nofink else." She graciously accepted him at his word and led him to the library and so resumed the weekly lesson of reading and writing. They never mentioned the letter of proposal that he wrote her. Things had gone back to the way they were.

After several months had gone by and at the end of the lesson Timothy said, "Sister, I won't be here next week. I'm going to America."

"You are going to America?" responded Sister Nicola with a rush of surprise.

"Yes. I've finally found the 'trouble and strife', sorry, the wife. I've found the wife. I'm going to ask her to let me go, divorce me. That way I can get on w'iv me life."

"Timothy, are you sure that's your only motive, you won't hurt her, will you?"

"Naw, I'm finished w'iv that business."

"I need to clear the air. I fought I'd write er a letter but the way I write, well it just wouldn't work. I'm taking me chances I know, but I'm going to see er."

"I'll pray for you Timothy."

"Lovely fanks. I need all the prayers I can get. I've never been on an airplane. I must say I'm a bit nervous, but I've got to sort this out, it's doing my head in. I've saved all me union pay for months and I've got enough for a ticket to New Orleans, Louisiana. Then I get a bus to

Covington. That's where she lives. I've already got me passport," he announced proudly.

"Good for you Timothy, I'm proud of you for dealing with this like a gentleman."

"It's only what you've shown me Sister Nicola."

"How did you find her?" He smiled at her and said,

"God works in mysterious ways Sister. After you told me to leave your family ome in Crowborough, I was devastated. I decided that I was going back on the 'Rob', nothing seemed to matter. I was casing a job with two of my old mates when I spotted a lad going into the dock gate. Even though I hadn't seen him for years I recognised him right away as Mary's boy, Jimmy. I grabbed hold of him took him to my flat and told him I wouldn't let him go until he told me where she was. He spilled the beans right away."

"You didn't hurt him, did you?"

"Naw, course not, didn't ave too."

"What about the job, the robbery?"

"I kept finking of all the fings that had happened to me, you coming to me in prison, the job, the way the foreman took care of me, the union job where I doubled my weekly wages. I started to fink that your God must ave ad his hand in this. So, I bottled out of the robbery. Good fing too, they never got the money. Someone spotted them sitting outside the dock gate and the old bill came, waited for them to do the deed and then took em both off to jail. They got done w'iv armed robbery. That is serious porridge, so they won't see the light of day for many a year. It's your God again I fink."

"I think he may be your God too." She beamed at him and hugged his arm. He could smell her and he felt his head swim.

The day came for the flight from Heathrow to Washington-Dulles airport and then from Washington-

Dulles to New Orleans International. Sister Nicola had prepared a traveling package for him with several sandwiches and a large jam filled sponge cake all wrapped in wax paper to keep it fresh. She also put in two packages of peanuts and two rather pitted apples. In addition, she gave him a new book to read by an American author named Billy Graham called Peace with God and he found it with a note. The note said; *No matter what, I'm so proud of you Timothy and the progress you have made and the gentleman you are becoming more every day.* He put the note to his nose for a slight whiff of her scent but all he could smell was the cheese and corned beef from the sandwiches.

The BA flight landed at Washington-Dulles airport and what hit him as he stepped off the plane, down the stairs and onto the tarmac was the heat and closeness of the air. He made his way into the terminal and bought a large bottle of beer and then a second because he was so thirsty. He felt drained and still dozy from the long sleep on the Atlantic leg of the flight. He looked for the half of the cheese and corned beef sandwich he had saved but he hadn't wrapped it thoroughly. It had become stale and the bread was dried out. He threw it out and bought a salmon salad sandwich on white bread. He enjoyed it so much that he purchased another and ate it. He found his way to his next gate for the flight to New Orleans. The flight to New Orleans was a relatively short one. He landed to a heat that was overwhelming and he started to sweat the minute he stepped off of the plane. He took off his jacket but it didn't matter. He had his first experience with the effects of heat and super high humidity. His shirt was soaking wet within minutes. Being in the same clothes for almost nineteen hours, sleeping in them and now the heat and humidity made him look even more intimidating than he normally did. He made his way to the taxi stand and asked how much to the Greyhound bus station. The price was reasonable. His pounds went a long way in America, much to his amazement. For every one of his English £1 he got nearly $5, U.S. He started to realize that he had more than enough for his one week stay in the U.S. The cab took him to the Greyhound station and he bought a two-way ticket to Covington, Louisiana. The bus left ninety minutes later. He was starting to get a little nervous and excited at the same time. In his mind he was wondering what kind of reaction that he'd receive after so many years. Would she still be afraid of him? Would her new man try to start something? He didn't worry too much about that part if there was anything Timothy Green could handle, it was physical violence.

The bus ride across Lake Pontchartrain was an epiphany. He'd never seen anything like this seemly neverending bridge that went on for mile after mile over the very shallow lake. Timothy thought from his vantage point in the bus that he could see to the bottom of the lake. He was gob-smacked. He couldn't help thinking, "*Blimey, this America is really something.*" He arrived in Covington late, after dark, and looked for a hotel. He found one fairly close to the bus station. It was seedy but it looked fine to Timothy as it was affordable. It had a bar of sorts downstairs, so after he settled and had a quick wash he went downstairs and had several beers. He spoke to the bartender, who sported long braided hair in a ponytail and a handlebar mustache.

Unlike Timothy he liked to chat, "So buddy, where you from?"

"England. Just arrived today. My first time ere."

"How do you like the good old U.S. of A?"

"Yeah, it's alright."

"Okay. How do you like our beer?"

"Tastes like weasel piss to me, and it's too cold mate."

"We Americans take our beer cold, dude".
"What did you call me?"
"I called you dude."
"I've never been called dude before. Mind if I use it; my mates back in England would get a kick out of me calling them all dude.
"It's a free country buddy use it all you want to, another beer?"
"Yeah, one more then I'm off to bed. I'm having trouble keeping my eyes open. "

****

He slept until eleven a.m. By the time he had a bath, shaved and got ready it was well after midday. He booked the room for another night and paid with cash. Then he went down and asked where to get a full English breakfast. The person at the front desk hadn't a clue what he was talking about.
"You know bacon and eggs."
"Oh, we serve breakfast all day in our diner."
"Where is the diner?" he asked. She pointed to the bar, and sure enough by day it was a café as he knew it and by night a bar. They served him bacon and eggs.
He complained at the kind of bacon they served him, "Oye this ain't real bacon. It's streaky bacon." He tried to explain that in England they had bacon with meat on it. The waitress was in her seventies and had heard it all in her day and was taking no guff from anyone including Timothy.
Finally, in frustration he said, "I'm not eating this streaky bacon. It's not fit for human consumption."
She responded with a wink and said, "Whatever blows your dress up honey pie." He started to laugh and

even though she looked like an old train wreck with too much makeup on, he liked her.

He finished his breakfast and left the bacon untouched. He asked the front desk where he could get a cab. The lady called a cab for him. He asked her if she'd ever heard of a bloke by the name of Jack Parker. The manager overheard the question and came out from the office behind the old beaten up reception counter.

"Yes I know Jack Parker. He is the manager of the local golf course. Is he a friend?"

"Not exactly," answered the big man, "I'm meeting him today for the first time." He smiled at the manager, walked out of the front entrance of the old hotel and jumped in the cab. He gave the address and asked the cabbie to drive to 1410 Nolan Road. The house was a large rancher style home on a semi industrial road but it was surrounded by live oak trees and a lot of unfamiliar looking southern foliage. It was two p.m. by this time and he asked the cabbie to wait. He went up to the door and found that he was uncharacteristically nervous. He knocked several times but no one came to the door. Timothy got back in the dusty cab and rode back to the hotel.

Timothy arranged with the cabbie to return at six that same evening. He was starting to wonder if this was worth all the effort he'd gone through but he wasn't going to back out now. He arrived at the house and someone was home. The lights were on. He asked the cab to wait and he went up to the door and knocked loudly. Mary walked to the front door. It was mostly a solid wooden door with a glass window in the top third of the door. Her eyes met his and she froze and started to back up slowly.

"Mary, I've come a long way to talk to you," he shouted so she could hear through the door. As she was backing up she tripped over a small hallway table and fell over. She jumped up quickly like she was a spring and ran to the phone. She dialed Jack's number.

He answered as usual, "Jack Parker."

She said quietly but very deliberately, "Jack it's me. He is at our front door and I'm getting the gun." She let the phone go and it thumped onto the floor. She ran to the bedroom and pulled open the top drawer of Jack's dresser. There it was the .44 Magnum. She grabbed it and didn't notice the weight from the adrenaline flowing through her veins. She looked for the safety and switched it off. The gun was now hot and she knew it. He knocked several more times.

"My husband will be here very soon," she shouted in a very shaky voice.

"I'm your bleedin husband," he said in frustration. "I want to talk to you but not through the door." She was shaking from head to toe and started to vibrate.

"He'll be here soon. He is on his way," Mary said with as much courage as she could muster.

"Open the door and talk to me will ya." He tried the door without thinking and to his shock it opened. There she was after all those years, looking older but still the same woman that he had married. She raised the gun. It was such a large gun it looked like a small cannon to the big man. He quickly slammed the door shut. He turned to walk away thinking to himself, "*This is nasty. I'm getting out of here. It's not worth my life.*" As he turned to leave a powder blue Ford Torino convertible pulled up into the yard. The driver slammed the car into park, which made the car rock back and forth. Out jumped Jack and raced to the spot where the big man stood. Jack was fast coming to the realization that he had underestimated just how big this man was. His size combined with all of the stories Mary had told him for all those years had instantaneously crashed down on Jack.

In that moment, he didn't know what to do. "I've come ere to talk to my wife and ask her to forgive me for what I did to er all those years ago and she nearly shot me. I want her to release me from this marriage and let me get on w'iv my life. That's all I'm ere for."

Jack was trembling and was having trouble processing this entire ridiculous scene. All he could think to do was to pray silently, *"Jesus, help me!" Then Jack's chin music kicked in.*

"My name is Jack Parker and Mary and I have been a couple for many years."

Timothy was relieved at Jack's reaction so he went to put out his hand out and that's when the door flung open.

Jack saw the gun and screamed, "No, Mary no!" A shot rang out. She was having trouble holding the heavy gun. She tried to pull out of the shot but it was too late. The bullet hit the cement post of the driveway pillar. The sound was deafening and shards of cement went everywhere. The cab screeched away in a hurry upon the sound of the gunshot.

Timothy let out a guttural cry and collapsed to the ground. "You've shot me Mary. You've shot me."

Jack raced to the front door to grab the gun from Mary. As he did she fainted and collapsed. He grabbed her from falling and carried her inside the house. With sirens blaring Sherriff Vance and his deputy pulled up in two separate vehicles and within moments of exiting their patrol cars had their guns drawn. Jack still had the .44 Magnum in his hand.

"Put the gun down Jack," came the stern command from Sheriff Vance. Jack dropped it immediately.

"What happened here?" asked Vance. The blood drained from Jack's head and all the air left him. He just sat on the step and put his head in his hands and had no idea what to do or say. "Would someone tell me what in the hell is going on here, or I'll be fixin to take you all in to custody?"

Timothy spoke first, "It was an accident. Mary was showing me her gun and the bloody fing went off. Just an accident, at's all it was." He was still on the ground bleeding from a very nasty shard of cement that had flown off the driveway post and punctured his right calf.

Jack came to his senses and said, "I'm sorry Vance. I shouldn't have called you. I really thought we were in trouble, but it turns out I couldn't have been more wrong."

"Is this the guy from the old country that you've told me about Jack?"

"Yes Vance, this is him but he is not here for the reason we believed he was. He came to make peace not war."

"I think I get it but I'll need to see the licence for that big man pistol that Mary 'accidently' almost shot her ex husband with. Come on Tyler let's get outta here and let these folks get on with whatever they need to get on with." His deputy, Tyler, didn't understand what was going on but he took direction from the sheriff. He jumped in his patrol car and drove away.

"You better get this big fellow to the doc's Jack. That's a nasty 'accident' he has suffered," he said in a sarcastic manner.

"Will do Vance, and thanks for your help."

"Yeah right," said the somewhat bewildered Louisiana law man.

"C'mon Tim let's get you to the hospital and get that leg looked at." Jack called a doctor friend that was a member at the course and an occasional golf partner of Jack's. Jack gave him the Readers Digest version of the evening's events and the doc agreed to meet them at the hospital and patch up Timothy's leg.

Jack put the gun away. He wanted to throw it away because of what could have happened. Mary was sitting on the couch and still vibrating from the fear of the entire situation. Jack poured her a small shot of bourbon and handed it to her.

"No thanks Jack. I hate the taste of whiskey."

"Mary, think of it as medicine. It will calm your nerves down and I'll be back from taking him to the hospital."

"Jack," she pulled him close to her and said, "please do not bring him back here."

"Okay, okay but I need to get him to the doc's. I'll be back soon."

Chapter #30 Forgotten

They pulled out of the yard in the blue convertible Ford Torino.

Jack asked him, "How are you doing?"

"Yeah alright. I'll be much better when they take this piece of cement out of me leg."

Jack couldn't help thinking, "*I hope he doesn't get any of that blood on my white leather seats.*"

It took *twelve* stitches to close the wound. The doctor handed Timothy the shard of cement and said, "You might want to keep this as a souvenir of your run in with a cement pillar."

As they left the hospital, Jack said "Tim, where would you like me to take you?"

"Back to your house. I must speak with Mary before I leave."

"She is very afraid of you and has asked me not to bring you back to the house." Timothy started to get angry but calmed himself down by thinking of what Sister Nicola would want him to do.

"Jack it's important. I really do want to be free of Mary and her of me. I fink she and you should be able to get on w'iv your lives. I need to get on w'iv mine mate. I don't want any trouble or cause her and you any agro."

"What?" said Jack, not understanding his lingo.

"Agro, aggravation," explained Timothy. "I treated Mary very poorly for many years and I want to be given the opportunity to apologize to her and ask for her forgiveness, w'ivout aving a gun pointed at me."

Jack laughed and then the big man laughed. Then they both laughed and somehow Jack couldn't help but like the man he'd been terrified of for too many years.

"Let's go to my place," said Jack. Mary was standing at the door when they rolled into the yard past the broken cement pillar. She was confused at seeing her tormentor sitting in the car with her Jack and they were smiling.

She looked at her man and said, "Jack?" He knew what she was saying to him without saying.

"Mary we need to clear the air."

"No Jack I will not after all those years sit with..."

"A man that's asking for forgiveness," said Timothy in a flat monotone voice. She froze and didn't know how *to respond.* "I'm glad you left me. Heaven knows what would have happened if you didn't. I was a mean and unpredictable man; I think I would ave hurt you".

His honestly touched her. After a few awkward seconds of silence, she finally looked at him and said, "Okay come in. Would you like a cup of tea?"

"Oh yeah I aven't ad one in three days. I could murder a good old cuppa tea". He couldn't help thinking his slang use of the word 'murder' was a little inappropriate in these circumstances. He asked about their lives and he admitted to holding Jimmy until he got their address. The big man then told his story and when he got to the part of his penguin, his face erupted in an unrelenting smile and his eyes sparkled.

Mary said, "You love this woman?"

"Yes," he confessed "but not in the way you might fink. She is a nun but she has been there for me for all these years, taught me to read and write, taught me that love is much better than hate. She's shown me God's love in practical ways. Between er and God they have kept me from a life of crime, even at times when I didn't want them too!"

Jack said, "Praise God from whom all blessings flow." Mary wondered if she had just witnessed the biggest miracle of her life, one that she could never have imagined in her wildest dreams. Several more cups of tea were consumed, and they visited and talked until well past midnight.

"Let me drive you home, or back to your hotel," said Jack.

"Fanks, it is getting late," said the big man.

Mary stood up and walked with the two men to the door and she hesitantly put out her hand and said, "Thank you."

Timothy took her hand in both of his and said, "Mary I'm truly sorry for all the arm I've done to you."

She just stood there in a state of utter shock. She said, "I cannot believe I'm saying this but as far as I'm concerned it's not just forgiven but it's forgotten." The big man was overcome and for only the second time that he could remember his bottom lip quivered. Then he cried and walked out of the house to the car. Both men drove to the old wooden hotel without a word.

Timothy got up the next day, late again. He stumbled down to the diner for a very late breakfast. The old waitress was there and she called him honey pie and she told him he'd get used to the bacon.

He laughed at her and said, "I don't fink so love." She laughed and told the other old waitress, "Hey that big fella called me love. I think I got myself an admirer." Timothy ate his food and thought he'd go back up to his room and read the book that Nicola had given him. He still had three days before his flight went back to Heathrow. He went to the front desk and asked to book and pay for the rest if his time in Covington.

The receptionist said, "I have a message for you Mr. Green." On a slip of paper, it read, "I'll pick you up for supper at six p.m., Jack."

Jack showed up at the old dilapidated hotel at six p.m. on the dot. The big fella was waiting at the front door. The powder blue convertible, with white seats and the top down made Timothy feel very important.

"Oye, fanks for having me over for me supper," said Timothy.

"No siree pal, we are pushing the boat out. We going to the club for dinner."

"This is a beautiful motor car," said the Englishman.

Jack laughed and responded, "You British and your 'motor *car*', it's just car."

"Ere, speaking of British, I've never seen anyone in England dress as flashy as you Jack. You take the bleedin cake mate."

"Timmy, my man, I'm going to take that as a compliment." They both started to laugh and they laughed all the way to 1410 Nolan Road. They picked up Mary and made their way to the golf club. Timothy Green was sure that was the most posh night he ever had. He felt out of place but Jack made sure he felt as welcome as he could. The big man really liked Jack, just as everyone did. Jack made him laugh and they just had to look at each other and they started laughing. At times neither of them even knew why. The next night Jack and Mary had Timothy to the house for supper and Jack gave him a Bible as a gift.

Timothy said, "Blimey, I can't get away from God. He's everywhere."

Jack looked at him and said, "Yes Timmy pal, I think you are being pursued by the Hound of Heaven." Timothy didn't answer him but thought of the love of his life, Sister Nicola.

The trip back was long but it was an overnight flight. He slept for most of the flight. When he arrived in London his leg was still very sore and it caused him to limp rather badly. He deplaned and was walking slowly toward the underground station to get back to the London's East end. As he did he thought he saw a flash of gray like a nun's habit standing behind a giant pillar in the main foyer of the airport. He went as fast as he could but it was just a lady in a long gray dress. As he turned the corner, there she was, Nicola without her habit. "Is it really you?" He beamed from ear to ear, and she noticed his limp.

"Oh Timothy, what on earth!" "She shot me, Mary shot me." Nicola's mouth dropped open in disbelief. "Let me tell you the story over a cup of tea."

They sat at the airport café and drank tea until he couldn't drink another drop. Hours went by and he told the entire unbelievable story.

"Jack is a Christian. Like you he's very committed to God. E's a real good bloke." Finally he plucked up the nerve to ask her why she wasn't wearing her habit.

"I will always love God with all my heart but I've felt for some time that perhaps it's time to open my heart to a different kind of love." Timothy Green cried again for only the third time in his life that he could remember.

Chapter # 31 Back to Hill country

"Hello this is Shirley Parker." "Hello Shirley, my dear. Listen I wanted to tell you that Jack has been offered a job in San Antonio at a brand-new golf club called Woodlands. It's on the east side of Highway 1604. If we move back to the Texas hill country we'll be close to you. We can get together for weekends and dinners. It will be like old times my dear Shirley."

"Mary I want you and Jack to consider moving back to the ranch. I'll move into the bunk house. I put in running water last year. You two can take over the big house. It will mean a thirty-minute commute for that nephew of mine but then you and I can spend lots of time together. You really are the daughter I never had. Please consider the offer."

"Oh Shirley, I love you. Of course we will. I'll speak with Jack about it."

"How was your trip back to England and seeing all of your family?"

"Wonderful. It was full of love and familiar faces and places. Shirley, it warmed the cockles of my heart,"

"Mary, what are the cockles of your heart?"

Mary laughed and said, "I haven't the faintest idea."

"Did you see Jimmy?"

"Yes."

"When is he coming back home?"

"Not sure. He's met a girl, a hairdresser named Susan. I think he's smitten."

The End!

Postscript

This is my second novel. The first was 'The Clock', a historical story based on truth. This book is a fictional story. However, James Hunter Yeoman did lead Queen Victoria's funeral procession. He did fight in the Great War and the Boer War. His wife's name was Mary and she was Jewish. They did have Georgie, Dora, Lily, Maud, Eva and Chris and two other children Richard and James. They were all very much as I've described them only even lovelier. They did have a Granddaughter named Mary and she did have a difficult life but despite it all became a somewhat celebrated landscape artist in North America.

Jack Parker lives in Boerne Texas and he is a character to put it mildly. He was a professional gambler. He won and lost several fortunes and may well again. He's presently in his 80's. Jack did turn to God in his later years and he tells everyone he meets about his hope!

Timothy Green doesn't exist; he is my imagining of a man found and made from a lack of love and then turned because of it.

The rest of the story is an amalgam of experiences and people that I've meet growing up in London's East End and in North America. I hope you enjoyed reading it. If you did please take a minute and let me know, I'd love to hear from you.

James Leslie Payne
paynesonjim@gmail.com